# A Sprinkle of Treachery

## The Pobyd Perfections Bakery Series

A Pinch of Change (Novella)

A Drizzle of Magic

A Splash of Arcana

A Dash of Sorcery

A Smidgen of Chaos

A Sprinkle of Treachery

A Dusting of Alchemy

A Coating of Conjuring

A Glaze of Trickery

A Dollop of Spellwork

An Icing of Wizardry

# A Sprinkle of Treachery

S. Usher Evans

Sun's Golden Ray Publishing

Pensacola, FL

Version Date: 5/23/26

ISBN: 978-1-965767-37-5



Map by Fred Kroner of Stardust Book Services
Cover Design and Chapter Typography by Sun's Golden Ray Publishing
Cupcake Line Art by Clara Fang
Line Editing by Danielle Fine, By Definition Editing
Proofreading by Lisa Henson, Capital Editing Services

Sun's Golden Ray Publishing
Pensacola, FL
www.sgr-pub.com

For ordering information, please visit
www.sgr-pub.com/orders

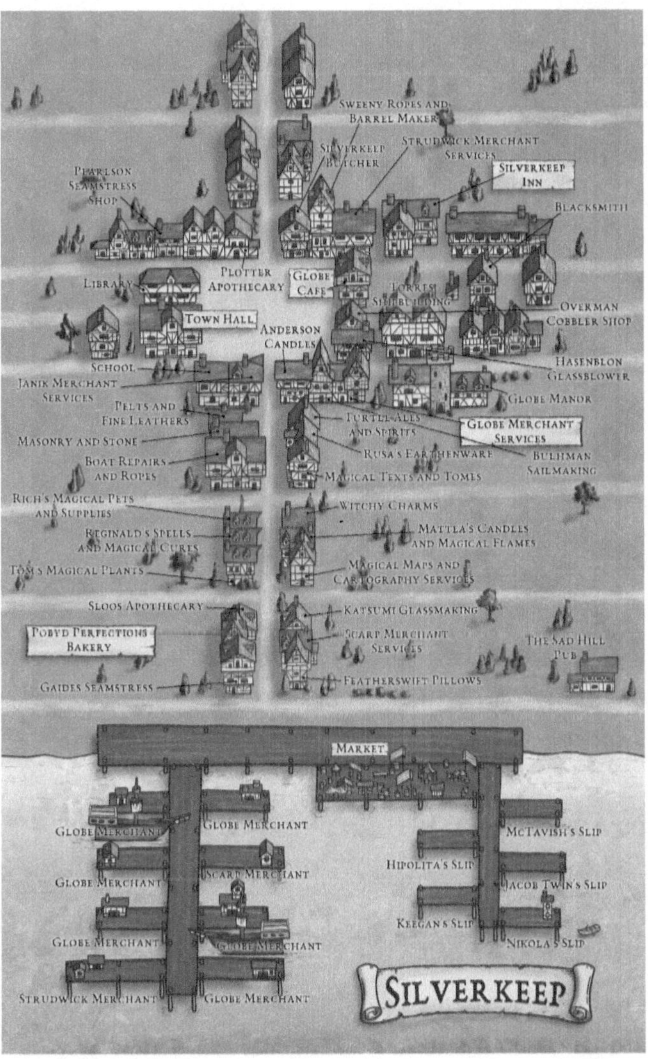
Sweeny Ropes and Barrel Maker
Silverkeep Butcher
Strudwick Merchant Services
Silverkeep Inn
Pearlson Seamstress Shop
Blacksmith
Plotter Apothecary
Globe Cafe
Library
Torres Shipbuilding
Overman Cobbler Shop
Town Hall
Anderson Candles
Hasenblon Glassblower
School
Janik Merchant Services
Globe Manor
Pelts and Fine Leathers
Turtle Ales and Spirits
Globe Merchant Services
Masonry and Stone
Rusa's Earthenware
Bulhman Sailmaking
Boat Repairs and Ropes
Magical Texts and Tomes
Rich's Magical Pets and Supplies
Witchy Charms
Reginald's Spells and Magical Cures
Mattea's Candles and Magical Flames
Tom's Magical Plants
Magical Maps and Cartography Services
Sloos Apothecary
Katsumi Glassmaking
Pobyd Perfections Bakery
Scarp Merchant Services
The Sad Hill Pub
Gaides Seamstress
Featherswift Pillows
Market
Globe Merchant
Globe Merchant
McTavish's Slip
Hipolita's Slip
Globe Merchant
Scarp Merchant
Jacob Twin's Slip
Keegan's Slip
Globe Merchant
Globe Merchant
Nikola's Slip
Strudwick Merchant
Globe Merchant
Silverkeep

"So we're talking three events total? One initial discussion, one meeting with the mayors, and the final vote?"

Lillie Dean, magical baker and owner of the Pobyd Perfections Bakery, sat with the two co-leads of the Silverkeep Fisherfolk Council, Jan and Orxan McTavish, discussing a potentially massive order. The McTavishes were already huge supporters of the bakery, assuming Lillie had at least one lemon-flavored good in the display case, but this would be creating cakes, cookies, and other delicious treats for the upcoming Fisherfolk Council Election—and would put a sizable amount of gold into Lillie's savings.

"Kemp Abora wanted to combine the mayoral election vote with the Fisherfolk one at the town hall in a few days," Jan said. "We can put your name in for catering, but I don't know who's in charge of that."

"Noted. Two events is more than enough." Lillie was practically giddy at the thought. "So what kind of sweets are we thinking?"

The two shared a look, and Jan shrugged. "I'm open to whatever you suggest—as long as—"

"There's a lemon-flavored pastry for you," Lillie said. *And those pastries lack any sort of magic.* "Let's see… What are we expecting for the first event? Is it a sit-down sort of thing, or will we be milling about?"

"The latter," Orxan said with a nod. "So probably something that isn't so messy."

"Agreed." Lillie thought for a moment. "Let's do a plate of cookies, for sure. Maybe some tartlets—small enough for one bite. And a dozen cupcakes, too, for something a little larger. How does that sound?"

"Perfect," Orxan said. "Jan?"

"No complaints here. For the second event, it's more sit-down, so we could do with a larger, sliceable cake," Jan said. "With maybe something lemon-flavored on the side?"

"Lemon cupcakes could work," Lillie said. "Yes, this is absolutely all doable."

"Thank goodness your oven is working again, Lillie," Jan said. "We were starting to panic a little. We weren't sure how we'd feed all these ornery fisherfolk."

Lillie couldn't have agreed more. It had really only been four days without her beloved oven, and most of those days had been dedicated to figuring out who was planting gigantic mushrooms to destroy the shops on the other side of town. And also... She wasn't going to think of those heart-stopping moments with Julian Globe. Especially not in front of her clients.

"I'll be there to set up about an hour before," Lillie said, checking her list to make sure she'd asked all the right questions. Quantity, time, flavor requests. "Do we need to worry about drinks? Plates and utensils?"

"No, Clifton—the bartender at the Sad Hill—he'll be handling that for us," Jan said. "He's got all the silverware and plates and stuff, too. It's not his first time hosting an event for us."

"Got it." Lillie'd had very few interactions with him, but he'd never struck her as overly friendly. "Is he all right with me bringing things?"

"Of course he is." Orxan waved her off.

"And if he isn't, you let us know," Jan said with a nod. "You're welcome to stick around and hear the speeches if you like. You're not fisherfolk, of course, but anyone who does business at the wharf can vote."

Lillie gave them a sideways look. "Really? Isn't this about dock slips?"

Orxan shook his head. "No, we're discussing all the business of the wharf. Of course, the big merchants like Mr. Globe don't attend, but the smaller merchants like Jeremias Scarp can come and make sure we know they get to keep their slips." He chuckled. "But it's rare we make any changes. Everyone who's got a spot usually keeps it. The election is more of a formality."

Lillie nodded. She'd not been too into the politics of the Fisherfolk Council, as she'd been busy with other problems in town recently. Her general understanding was there was limited space where fisherfolk and merchants could bring their ships to load and unload cargo. Mr. Globe, and his massive Globe Merchant Services, took up the lion's share of the spots. Two other dock slips apiece had been *graciously* provided to Jeremias Scarp and May Janik, and the last little bit had been set aside for the fisherfolk. There were more fisherfolk than slips, and there was often jockeying for position amongst those who desired a spot—usually given to those who were the most adept at fishing.

Her neighbor, Nikola Koven, was the top fisherfolk producer, partially due to her magical lineage, which wasn't known to anyone else. The fisherfolk were mostly anti-magic, spurred on by Jan and Orxan, the former of whom went to great pains to hide their bright pink wings from everyone. Lillie had discovered the fisherfolk's secret when she'd first moved to town, and there was a mutual understanding that anything lemon-flavored would be void of pobyd magic and safe for Jan to eat.

"I'm glad to hear you aren't expecting much excitement," Lillie said, closing her notebook. "I'm not sure I'll be needed to give an opinion, but I have no complaints about any of the farmers who sell down at the wharf market."

"Well, the invitation is there, and you're absolutely welcome," Orxan said. "But we do need to be getting back down to the wharf. The market doesn't stop because of the council's activities."

"No, it doesn't," Jan said with a heavy sigh. "And goodness knows, Jarvis Collin is making enough noise to make me think he's going to try to run for our spot."

"I can't believe they're doing both elections at the same time," Lillie said with a grimace.

"Ours is a four-year cycle," Jan explained. "And the mayor…well, we can't help that the mayor retired now, can we?"

"Not as if we saw hide nor hair of him at all," Orxan said. "But Mr. Abora did a good job of doing all the work."

Lillie grinned tightly. There hadn't actually been a mayor of Silverkeep in quite some time, just Mr. Abora doing Mr. Globe's bidding. She *still* wasn't sure how they got that by the queen's uptight election monitors, but she suspected Mr. Globe had paid a lot of gold for them to look the other way.

"He's the only one running, so I understand," Lillie said. "That should make it easy."

"Well, you know, with all the magicals and non-magicals popping up out of the woodwork, you never know who's thinking they can do a better job." Orxan shook his head. "Not me, I'll tell you that much. Everyone's got an opinion about how to run things until they're actually running it. Then it's a whole different kettle of fish."

~

The McTavishes bade Lillie farewell (with a chocolate chip cookie and lemon macaron each), leaving her to the business of running a bakery. She did a quick inventory of her display cases before the afternoon rush, ensuring she had enough to satisfy the cravings of her usual customers. As soon as Lillie had finished rearranging the plates of confections, a colorful bob of hair passed the window and let herself inside, followed by a nervous, and more importantly, *human*-looking man. Human-looking folks were obviously common around Silverkeep, but this particular one had had the head of a shark until very recently—and Lillie was pleased to see that the broken curse was still holding, which meant his brother was still sitting in a jail cell somewhere far away.

"Tom," Lillie said with a grin. "Look at you, out and about."

Tom grinned, casting a nervous look at Wineke, who slapped him on the back lovingly.

"I know, right?" Wineke said. "I keep trying to tell him that he looks normal now—well, you know, not *normal*, but not... Well, the teeth, and—"

"I get it, I get it." Lillie laughed. "You really should be enjoying all that Silverkeep has to offer, Tom."

"I've made it one more block than yesterday," he said with a sheepish grin. "Which is to say that Wineke threatened not to buy my latest batch of dried yellow lady's slippers if I didn't accompany her for her afternoon pastry." He peered through the glass cover. "And gosh, I haven't seen such a collection before. These all look scrumptious."

Lillie beamed. "They taste pretty good, too."

"Oh, don't be bashful," Wineke chided. "They're the most delicious pastries in all of

Silverkeep."

Tom hemmed and hawed over his choice, but when Wineke suggested that they get something different and share, he jumped on that immediately. They sat with a chocolate scone and a lemon curd-filled croissant and got to work divvying the treats up between them.

"Oh, goodness," Tom said, looking down at the croissant. "This is outrageous. The most… How did you…? And the lemon!"

"You've obviously never had a pobyd-baked pastry before," Wineke said, taking a big bite of the chocolate scone. "Oh, Lillie, you've outdone yourself on these." She broke off a piece and gave it to Tom, but he shook his head.

"I can't. This is too… I'm going to be back here every day, I'd wager," he said, swallowing. "Oh, dear, this is such a terrible discovery."

"So you're a fan of lemon?" Lillie asked. "Jan McTavish is, too, so I've always got something lemony in stock for them."

"McTavish…" Wineke reached into her pocket and pulled out a stack of cards, flipping through them. "Ah! Jan and Orxan McTavish. Fisherfolk. They run the council, don't they?"

"Yes, but…what in the world are those?" Lillie asked.

"These are my cards for all the important people

in Silverkeep I need to know about."

Lillie chuckled. "And why do you need to know about important people?"

"Oh! I haven't told you yet, have I?" Wineke adjusted her tunic as if she were about to deliver a speech. "I'm running for mayor."

Lillie's brows shot up. "What?"

"Yes!" Wineke beamed. "You know, that awful Mr. Abora is always on Mr. Globe's side, and the transplants', too. It's high time we had some magical representation."

"I...see..." Lillie tilted her head. "What does Greeley say about that?"

"Greeley's not running, I am. And with Fawn helping, he barely needs me anymore anyway." She shifted in her seat. "Besides that, I think once he gets used to the idea, he's going to be very happy to have me in power."

Lillie could only imagine Greeley's response. The apothecary was a bit set in his ways and always worried Wineke was getting herself in trouble when she would follow along with Lillie's investigations. Hearing Wineke was putting herself out there as mayor...

"So, you're friendly with the McTavishes?" Wineke said, jotting that down on her cards.

"Friendly enough," Lillie said. "Why?"

"Well, in Silverkeep, there are three main

factions, aren't there?" Wineke said. "The transplants, the returned, and the fisherfolk. The returned are *probably* going to throw their weight behind Mr. Abora, you know. And the magicals, well..." She pointed to herself. "Loyalty and all that. So the only real battleground is going to be the fisherfolk. They don't seem to fit in with the returned, but they're not quite magical."

Lillie nodded slowly.

"So if I can get the endorsement of the McTavishes, maybe that'll sway enough of 'em to vote for me," Wineke finished.

"There's an election event happening tomorrow night," Lillie began.

"Well, I obviously can't go unless I've been invited," Wineke said. "It would look like I'm fishing for votes. But maybe you could go and, I don't know, chat with some of the fisherfolk and see where their loyalties lie? Maybe mention that I'm running, too."

Lillie sighed. "I've been invited, but—"

"Oh, brilliant!" Wineke grinned, jumping to her feet. "You really are a wonderful friend. I'll be by with some campaign materials as soon as Reginald finishes duplicating them. And then we can talk about my platform!"

She scampered around the corner, planted a kiss on Lillie's cheek, then dashed out of the store before

Lillie could get a word in edgewise, leaving Lillie and Tom to stare at each other in stunned surprise.

"I suppose I'm going to the fisherfolk council meeting," Lillie said after a moment.

"I'll second what Wineke said about you being a wonderful friend," Tom said, rising slowly. "Especially since, erm, I haven't gotten any visits from Sheriff Juno or the shopkeepers in the town square."

"And I don't think you will," Lillie said softly with a smile. Tom had only known about his brother's evil deeds, and while a case could be made that he was somewhat guilty, Lillie had seen the remorse in his eyes. "I'm glad to see Ned remains safely behind bars."

At the mention of his brother's name, Tom shuddered. "They sent me a letter, you know. The King's people. I suppose they wanted to let me know why they'd taken my brother prisoner. But I wrote back and told 'em to keep him with an explanation of all he'd done to me over the years. It was very cathartic." He chuckled. "Imagine my surprise when I got a response saying my comments would most likely extend his sentence. Apparently, cursing one's brother to look like a shark runs afoul of several laws and regulations around magic use."

Lillie beamed. "Good. Serves him right. In the meantime, I hope you enjoy this peaceful time.

Make new friends. Explore the world."

"I surely will, Lillie." He took her hands and shook them. "Thanks to you."

"I didn't actually do anything, except spare Mr. Globe a costly repair bill," Lillie said with a shrug. In fact, Mr. Globe had been quite clear that her involvement had resulted in one gold coin struck from the hundred she owed him.

"You gave me the confidence to stand up to him," Tom said. "That's worth more than anything else in the world."

~

Lillie sent him on his way with another lemon pastry then tended to the usual rush of afternoon customers who stopped in after a long day at the wharf. There was lots of talk about the upcoming fisherfolk elections, as well as some more scuttlebutt about how Jarvis Collin was thinking about throwing his hat in the ring. Abraham Roudie, who worked as a dockhand, was particularly annoyed by this turn of events, as he considered it a betrayal of all the McTavishes had done for the fisherfolk.

"And if you think Audo Globe is going to work with a man like Jarvis, you're dreamin'," he railed to his friend Keegan Curtis, one of the fisherfolk.

"We'll have to see," Keegan replied with a shrug.

The crowd died down as the sun sank. A refreshing breeze slipped in through the open bakery door, reminding Lillie that the seasons were changing. This far south, summer had held on as long as possible, but finally, the first inklings of fall were starting to make their appearance.

She was about to close when a figure darkened her door. "Ms. Dean. So glad to see you're back to work."

Mr. Calcut was Lillie's merchant for all the unusual things she couldn't get down at the wharf, like chocolate, cinnamon, leavening, and cream of tartar. He was a bit mysterious, and Lillie still didn't have the full measure of him, but she did know he liked her, and he was always willing to cut her a deal.

Tonight, though, she had something rather important to ask him—and she was a little nervous about it.

"Your gold, and the back payment for the last shipment," Lillie said with a nod. "Thank goodness Yosepha was able to get my oven back to normal quickly."

"Indeed." Mr. Calcut swiped the bag off the table then frowned. "This is far more than you owe me, Ms. Dean."

"Yes, well." She smoothed her apron. "I wanted to see about a…new deal. Please, feel free to decline, and we can go back to what we were doing before."

He met her gaze, amusement sparkling in his

dark eyes. "Go on."

"I know that you and Julian Globe have had a disagreement, and Julian has, erm…" Lillie probably should've practiced this. "Well, he wants to buy from me. So if it's all right with you, I can—"

"Double your order, sell it to Mr. Globe, then pocket the profit?" He tilted his head.

"I understand this might not be a deal you want to make," Lillie said quickly. "Which is why I wanted to be upfront about it. You've been such a wonderful business partner that I don't want to anger you."

He surveyed Lillie for a moment, and she honestly had no idea what was going on in his mind. "I was curious when Mr. Globe cancelled his usual order with me without explanation. But my real concern is why he'd be willing to let you pocket the difference?"

She swallowed. How could she put this in so that it wouldn't reveal *everything*? "Julian, being a good friend, thought it would be a mutually beneficial arrangement. I could pocket a little extra, and he could get a slightly better deal on his goods."

"And I would be cut out of the deal."

Lillie's eyes widened. "If it doesn't suit you, I'm very happy to—"

"No, no. In fact, I don't mind having one less stop to make." He chuckled. "And I honestly have to commend the man for finding a solution that both makes him a better profit and also potentially enrages his father. I know how much Julian enjoys doing the latter." He bowed and produced another bag from his pocket. "I assume you'll get this where it needs to go?"

"Absolutely." Lillie shifted from side to side. "And if it's not too much trouble, if you wouldn't mind…not mentioning this to anyone? Julian might be fine with enraging his father on a regular basis, but I'm not."

He nodded. "Discretion is my middle name. Shall we increase the delivery frequency as well?"

"If you don't mind," Lillie said. "Every four days sound good?"

"See you in four days."

Lillie made quick work of divvying up the supplies evenly, keeping half the chocolate, cinnamon, and other spices for herself and bundling the rest in a bag. She left the supplies outside the back door, debating if she should put a bucket over it to keep the animals away. But the only menace she'd ever seen around these parts was a raccoon that turned out to be her neighbor, so she decided to leave it as it was.

In the morning, Lillie opened her door to find not only a small sack of gold, but a letter. A goofy grin grew on her face as she brought both inside, ripping off the wax seal on the envelope and hungrily inhaling the words.

Dear Lils,

I hope this letter finds you well. I'd already cancelled my order with Mr. Calcut, so I hope I can deliver this to you and get my supplies this evening. If not, then I hope this letter will brighten your day.

It's been boring here without you baking with me. I find myself getting up too early and wandering my kitchen, looking for you. I've started keeping the spoons in that one drawer, where you'd put them. To be truly honest, I keep wishing for another calamity to befall Silverkeep so I can look into your beautiful brown eyes again.

Odetta has been banned from seeing me, so my days are quite lonely. But I have a feeling once things die down a bit, my father might start looking the other way again when she sneaks out to visit. The election is starting to take up a lot of his attention, as he's decided against Mr. Abora and chosen Clancy Cast, the butcher, as his new candidate. He's paid a lot of money to bring in a new campaign manager and her assistant, so I'm sure he feels he's got it in the bag.

You are constantly in my thoughts. I hope this new harebrained scheme will get us to our first date sooner than later.

Yours,

J

Lillie couldn't help the sigh that escaped her lips. She leaned against her kitchen table as she read through it slower, languishing on his declarations of affection and how much he missed her. She was eternally grateful her landlord, Reynard Moussison

VIII, wouldn't wake up for a few more hours, because if anyone saw her in this state, they would surely question why she had hearts in her eyes.

She read the last line about their *first date* again before pressing the letter to her chest. Julian had all but asked her out the last time they'd spoken, and while Lillie wanted nothing more than to pursue a relationship with him, she had used the debt to his father as an excuse to slow things down.

That wasn't the entire truth, though. Mr. Globe had *also* used his considerable influence to find out Lillie's history in Lower Pigsend. She'd nearly exposed three thousand innocent magical souls to the wrath of the queen after stealing the protective talisman that kept everyone hidden so she could escape the enclave. It had been reckless and selfish, and Lillie couldn't imagine what her friends would think of her if they knew.

"A problem for another day," Lillie said, carefully folding the letter and storing it with her most precious items in a drawer in the front room. It was time to get to work.

The Fisherfolk Council would be commencing around five in the afternoon, which meant Lillie could spend the morning filling her display cases and use her afternoon baking time to work on the McTavishes' pastry tray. Kristin Honeygold, her dairy farmer friend, would be by around six with the day's shipment, but she had a few jugs from yesterday's delivery to work with until then.

Despite her promise to Tom to always have something lemony, she set aside her crate of lemons for the later bakes, instead choosing to make cinnamon chip scones with her new shipment from Mr. Calcut. She started by melting sugar on the stove until it was boiling then added the cinnamon and a bit of salt.

She poured that mixture out onto a tray and leaned over to whisper, "Dry out, please."

The sugar-cinnamon mixture complied immediately, turning brittle and crumbly. Lillie set that tray aside to work on the scones themselves. But before she could dig her fingers into the flour and butter, there was a quiet rap at the back door.

Lillie's heart leapt to her throat. Julian?

But when she opened the door, she found none other than Nikola Koven, looking a little nervous.

"Nikola, good morning," Lillie said, stepping aside to let her neighbor in. "Is everything all right?"

"Oh, yes. All is well. I just..." Was the even-keeled fisherfolk actually flushing? "Goodness, this is so embarrassing to ask, but Ursil is such a dear, and..."

"You can tell me," Lillie said patiently. "Whatever it is, I promise I'm happy to listen."

"Well." She inhaled. "It's our anniversary in a

few days. Ten years, if you can believe it."

Lillie clapped happily. "Congratulations! Would you like me to bake something for you?"

Nikola nodded. "Except, well, I remember..." She cleared her throat. "I'm not the most romantic of people. Ursil's always the one who... I mean, you've met him."

Lillie had to laugh. "Of course."

"I wanted this to be special for him, and I remembered when you, erm..." She tilted her head to the side. "Did the thing. With that cookie. The mind-control thing."

Lillie scowled, some of her bubbly happiness evaporating with the memory. "It wasn't *mind control*. It was encouragement to tell the truth."

Encouragement because *someone* had been dropping nasty blackmail letters at her door, and Lillie had thought it was Benetta Pearlson, the other person in town who knew about Lillie's past mistake. Lillie had made a batch of cookies laced with truth-telling magic, but thankfully, she'd come to her senses before Benetta ate one.

"Right. Encouragement. That's the word I was looking for." Nikola ran her hands down her tunic as if they were sweaty. "Can you add some of that to a chocolate cake covered in strawberries?"

"Encouragement for what?" Lillie asked.

"Well, erm... Romance, I guess? I don't know.

You're the expert, right?" Nikola looked *most* uncomfortable. "I told you it was embarrassing."

"Not at all," Lillie said, waving her off. "As a general rule, I don't like using that sort of magic, but I'm happy to for you and Ursil. You've been nothing but kind to me since I moved in."

Nikola beamed, some of her angst disappearing. "I was hoping to keep it a little bit of a surprise for Ursil, too."

"Say no more." Lillie held up her hands. "My lips are sealed. Chocolate cake with strawberries, you said?"

Nikola nodded. "I think that's his favorite. I can pick it up three days from now, in the afternoon, if you aren't too busy."

"For you? Anything."

~

Between Julian's letter and the early morning order from Nikola (and accompanying gold coin), Lillie couldn't help but grin as she went about the rest of her morning. Even Rey was curious about Lillie's excellent mood when he came out of his mousehole for his daily pastry.

"Just happy to be back to baking," Lillie said, trying her darnedest to wipe the smile off her face. "And we've had a few days of calm."

"We'll see how long that lasts, with the mayoral election getting into full swing," Rey said.

"Apparently, the scuttlebutt now is that Mr. Globe no longer has confidence in Mr. Abora. He's got Clancy Cast—the butcher—as his candidate now."

"You don't say," Lillie said, feigning innocence. "What does Mr. Abora think about all this?"

"Well, he's actually been dining frequently at the Silverkeep Inn," Rey said. "Which you know he never does. It's been so awkward."

"Why?"

"Nobody likes him, and seeing as most of the folks who frequent the Silverkeep Inn are Mr. Globe's tenants… I mean, they're not going to vote against the guy their landlord told them to vote for. But Kemp is trying anyway."

"They might," Lillie said. "Have any of them said they're voting for Wineke?"

Rey tilted his head. "Is she running?"

"So she tells me," Lillie said. "I don't think Greeley is too pleased about it, but you know how she can be."

"Ah, well. I don't think she can count on the Silverkeep Inn vote," Rey said. "But that's such a small portion of the town these days. There's the merchant contingent, the fisherfolk, and I assume Wineke has the magical folks in the bag, too."

"Probably." She didn't know anyone who didn't love her. "Do the small folk get a vote?"

"We could probably lobby for one, I suppose,"

Rey said thoughtfully. "But it's never been an issue. The big folks have their business, and the small folk have ours. Not much overlaps."

Their conversation was cut short by the sound of the door opening, but instead of Wineke or even Tom, Mr. Abora stood on the threshold, looking quite unnerved to be there. The assistant mayor was tall and thin, with his long black hair always braided down his back. For a man in charge of the town, he was often jumpy, and he never seemed to want to be in one place for long.

"Mr. Abora," Lillie said with a smile as she wiped her hands and came out to the front room. "To what do I owe the pleasure?"

"Ah, Ms. Dean. Lillie, if I may." He flashed her a grin that was all politics. "I had a rather large favor to ask you."

"Sure," Lillie said. *As long as it comes with a rather large sum of gold...*

"Well, I'm sure you've heard that the election is heating up," Mr. Abora said. "I hope I can count on your vote."

Lillie licked her lips, glancing toward the wall that separated her shop from Wineke's. "I'm not sure you can. Wineke is a dear friend and—"

"And a magnificent apothecary," Mr. Abora finished. "But being mayor is more complex than mixing potions. Lots of politics to consider, especially with all the topsy-turviness of things out of King's Capital."

Lillie wasn't really keen to discuss her vote. "You mentioned you needed a favor?"

"Ah, yes, well, I'd like to ask if you're available to cater an event for me," he said. "A little campaign rally at the town hall. It'll give the citizens of Silverkeep a chance to get to know the real me."

"Not the fake assistant mayor who's been covering for a mayor who never existed on behalf of Mr. Globe?" Rey asked sweetly.

Lillie glared at him. "Behave."

Mr. Abora cleared his throat. "Precisely. It would be amazing if you could provide some cookies, or even a cake. Something delectable that would put everyone in a good mood."

"And you don't want to ask Julian because...?" Lillie wasn't about to look a gift horse in the mouth, but it did strike her as odd that Mr. Abora would come to her instead of the bakery next door.

"Well, erm, Mr. Globe—Audo, that is—and I aren't exactly on the best terms right now," Mr. Abora said. "And I thought it would be a nice show of unity to have the magical baker provide some refreshments. That's what my campaign is all about, you see. Unity!"

Lillie nodded as she pulled her notebook from its hiding spot beneath her display counter. "Let's see. I've got the Fisherfolk Council to cater tonight, and they've asked me to do the mayoral chat two days after that." She tapped her charcoal against the page. "And your event would be tomorrow, right? That's perfectly doable. What sort of flavors are you looking for?"

"I'll leave that up to you," he said. "And I'm happy to pay you two gold coins for the effort."

Lillie jotted that down, trying to keep the joy off her face. "That's very generous."

"I know anything you make will be absolutely delicious—and the perfect boost to my campaign. Goodness knows I'm already fighting an uphill battle against Kathryn Harkness."

"Who?" Lillie frowned.

"Mr. Globe's campaign manager for Clancy," Mr. Abora said. "She's come all the way from King's Capital for some reason. I suppose he wanted to make sure I knew he'd lost faith in my abilities."

"Or he doesn't have much faith in Clancy," Lillie said.

"Oh, he *definitely* doesn't," Rey chimed in. "I'm pretty sure he drew a name out of a hat. Not as if that person's going to be making many decisions themselves, am I right, Mr. Abora?"

"Quite." Mr. Abora shifted uncomfortably.

"The people of Silverkeep can look beyond a fancy name," Lillie said. "They'll know who they can trust."

Before Mr. Abora could answer, the door flung open, and Wineke, now sporting very neutral sandy-blonde hair, barged in looking madder than a hornet's nest.

"What is *this*?" she bellowed. "Are you trying to poach my best friend, Abora?"

"Nobody's poaching anyone," Lillie said. "Mr. Abora is simply hiring me to cater an event."

Wineke glowered at him, and the assistant mayor had the good sense to wilt. "Is he now? I hope you told him to stuff it."

"Wineke, I'm not about to say no to business," Lillie said. *Especially not while I owe Mr. Globe.* "It's fine. Just because I'm catering an event doesn't mean I've made up my mind on who to vote for."

Wineke looked at her with a trembling lip. "B-but, Lillie—"

"Oh, stop it," Lillie scolded. "A vote is private for a reason, but that doesn't mean I won't support both your campaigns. Do you have those materials for the Fisherfolk Council? I'm happy to bring them by."

Wineke deposited the pamphlets on the table. "And you'll talk about me, right?"

"I will," Lillie said with a nod.

"I didn't realize we could do pamphlets," Mr. Abora said, picking up one of the pages. "How did you…?" He clicked his tongue. "The mage."

"Funny what happens when you've got friends who can do magic," Wineke said hotly.

Lillie needed to separate these candidates before Wineke lost the bakery order. "Mr. Abora, we're all set on your order," she said. "Is there anything else you need from me?"

There wasn't, though Wineke lingered a few minutes after Mr. Abora left to press Lillie on who she and Rey planned to vote for.

"I can't vote," Rey said, climbing down the display case. "But if I did, I would surely vote for you, Wineke."

"Thanks, Rey." Wineke turned to Lillie. "And you, dearest friend who lives next door? Are you going to vote for me?"

"Of course I'm voting for you," Lillie said, dropping her voice as if Mr. Abora could still overhear. "But I can't say that to someone who wants to pay me two gold coins to cater their election event, now can I?"

"Suppose not," Wineke said. "But you don't need his gold, do you?"

"I do, actually," Lillie said lightly, patting the flyers. "Now, I promise I'll get these to the campaign event, but if you don't skedaddle and let me start baking, I won't have anything to *bring* to the event."

"Okay, okay." Wineke beamed at her. "You're

the best, Lillie."

"I try."

Lillie bade her farewell and hurried into the kitchen, throwing on her apron—and it was at that precise moment that she realized she'd been too distracted by all the busyness of the morning to notice she hadn't had one *very* important visitor.

Namely, Kristin Honeygold, and three much-needed jugs of milk. She'd had plenty for the morning's bakes, so it hadn't even crossed her mind.

She frowned. It wasn't like Kristin to skip a delivery, especially knowing how Lillie would work through every jug of milk she brought in a single day.

"Hey, Rey," Lillie said, pulling off her apron, "I've got to run down to the wharf market. You haven't heard anything about Kristin, have you?"

"Kristin?" Rey emerged from his mousehole again. "No, I can't say I have. She didn't stop by?"

"No." Lillie tried to quell her unease. "I'm sure it's fine. I'll be back in a bit."

Lillie walked briskly toward the wharf market, where she'd find her produce, sugar, and other vendors. She hadn't needed to come to Kristin's booth in several weeks, and when she rounded the corner to it, she stopped short.

A very different face was sitting behind the jugs of milk: Kristin's sister, Esmerelda Honeygold.

Lillie winced. Esmerelda would've fit right in with the transplants, all of whom nursed a healthy hatred of all things magical. She'd never liked Lillie and Kristin's friendship, and that opinion hadn't seemed to change in the weeks since Lillie had been to their house in search of willow bark.

The elder Honeygold sister scowled as Lillie approached. "What do *you* want?"

"Well, for starters, I'd like to know if Kristin is well," Lillie said, gesturing to the booth.

Esmerelda eyed her, and Lillie could almost see the wheels turning in her head. Finally, she clicked her tongue, as if speaking to Lillie were beneath her. "Broke her leg."

"*What?*" Lillie gasped. "Is she all right? Goodness me, what in the world—?"

"Calm down. She's fine. Was trying to fix a broken shingle on the roof." Esmerelda tutted. "She can't get around. So I'm here doing her job, and my wife is doing the work of two people."

"You should have Reginald take a look at it," Lillie said.

"Who?"

"The mage—"

"Absolutely not." Esmerelda's brown eyes darkened. "There will be no magic of any sort in my home."

Lillie blinked. Esmerelda was vehemently anti-magic, as their parents had been taken away by the queen's people for raising magical sheep. She hadn't thought it fair that magical folks like Lillie had found refuge from the queen's people and had made it clear to Lillie that, while Kristin could do what she wanted, Esmerelda and her wife Charla did not want Lillie darkening their front door.

But to be so anti-magic that she'd deny medical help to her sister?

"I understand that you're not a fan," Lillie began gently. "But Kristin's hurt, and—"

"She's getting pain relief tinctures from the apothecary," Esmerelda snapped. "She's fine. Got lots of books to read and keep her company. She doesn't need *magic*."

Lillie ran her tongue along her teeth instead of arguing, deciding that, as soon as the McTavishes' baked goods were out the oven, Lillie would march right up to the farm to check on Kristin herself and, if need be, pay for Reginald to repair her leg.

"Very well. I need my milk order," Lillie said. "Kristin usually delivers it every morning on her way in. I've got a few things to bake this evening."

Esmerelda rolled her eyes and made a show of pawing through the crates. Then she pulled out one with a yellow ribbon on it and put it down on the table. "Two gold."

"Kristin and I usually do four jugs to make four pounds of butter," Lillie replied sweetly.

"Well, I don't eat that rancid butter, so it's two gold, or I'll sell these to someone else."

Luckily, Lillie had had the wherewithal to grab her coin purse, so she forked over the coins with a growl.

"A jug for a pound of butter. No wonder we aren't making any money," Esmerelda muttered. "And I'll thank you to pay that amount going forward. You're no longer allowed to barter like that with Kristin. We can't be giving milk away for free."

Lillie bit her tongue instead of reminding Esmerelda that Kristin usually sold that butter—and made twice as much as when it was milk. If Lillie wanted to check on Kristin before the Fisherfolk Council, she'd have to get a move on.

"I take it you won't be delivering to me in the morning," Lillie said with a sigh. "So I'll have to make a trip down here?"

"The Casts have a small dairy," she said. "Perhaps you should consider buying from them if you want concierge service."

Lillie glared at her and snatched the crate off the counter, mentally considering how much she'd be willing to pay Reginald to fix Kristin's leg so she wouldn't have to deal with Esmerelda again.

~

Lillie returned to the bakery in a huff. She was so put out that she almost overmixed the cookie dough and melted the chocolate chips. But as she busied herself with making a dozen cupcakes and arranging fruit on a few tartlets, her anger slowly evaporated, leaving only concern for Kristin's wellbeing. Her sister might not want to bring magic into her home, but Lillie wasn't about to let Kristin be laid up for weeks.

And not only because it meant Lillie would have to make an extra trip every morning.

First, though, Lillie needed to get these pastries to the Sad Hill Pub, because if she left that task for going to see the chatty Kristin, there was a good chance she'd be late. She employed three display platters to carry the pastries, arranging them nicely on each one so there would be a good mix, then pulled off her apron and went to seek help to carry everything.

Next door, Greeley and his mouse assistant Fawn were hard at work mixing potions.

"Ah, Lillie." Greeley smiled. "Wineke is out campaigning."

"Is she now?" Lillie frowned. "Do either of you have a moment to help me get these pastries down to the Sad Hill Pub?"

"Oh, I wish I could, but this potion is time-sensitive," Greeley said. "If you can wait half an hour—"

"Not to worry, I'll find someone else."

She had to poke around in three different stores (including Maire Gaides, the nonmagical seamstress on the other side of her shop, who all but threw Lillie out) before Haruko, the kitsune glassblower across the street, agreed to help. That is, she offered to get her boyfriend Reginald to help.

"I'm sure it'll be no trouble for him to charm the platters to float behind you," Haruko said, pulling a string over by the wall. A moment later, Reginald appeared with a small *pop* and grinned at Haruko before she pointed to Lillie. "She's the one asking for you, dear."

"Ah, Lillie, what can I help you with?" Reginald asked. "Oven's working all right, isn't it?"

"I actually have two things to ask," Lillie said. "First, would you mind charming a couple of platters to float behind me? I've got to deliver some goodies to the Fisherfolk Council discussion this evening over at the Sad Hill Pub."

"Absolutely," Reginald said. Then, when Haruko cleared her throat pointedly, he added sheepishly, "Erm, usually a charm is a gold."

*Ouch*, but worth it, in this case. The McTavishes had paid handsomely for Lillie's pastries, and she could afford it. "Well, that leads me to my second question. One of my dear friends, Kristin, seems to have broken her leg. I'm headed up there after dropping these off, and I wondered—"

"Oh, I don't go near broken bones," Reginald said, holding up his hands. "That's for a medical mage. Scrapes, bruises, absolutely. Sprains? That's pushing it. But bones require so much extra training."

Lillie deflated. "I see. Well, her sisters are anti-magic in the first place, so it was an uphill battle to even get you in the front door. Do you know of any medical mages around here?"

"Not in these parts, no," Reginald said with a shake of his head. "I'm sure Greeley could whip up a nice potion for her to expedite the healing, though."

"That's a thought," Lillie said, reaching into her pocket. "Here's the gold. The platters are over at the bakery. Appreciate the help!"

Reginald made quick work of the platters (and helped himself to a chocolate muffin, too), and before long, Lillie was climbing off the wooden planks of the wharf and onto the sandy beach, headed toward the Sad Hill Pub in the distance. It was even more of a ramshackle place in the light, leaning heavily against the winds that came off the ocean.

She opened the door, immediately struck by the lingering stench of ale and salt. Behind the counter, the bartender Clifton was wiping the counter with a dirty rag and glowered at Lillie as if she were an unwanted pest.

"You're early," he grunted. "Council won't be here until after five."

"I'm sure these can be out of the way in the back room or wherever we're meeting," Lillie said patiently, gesturing to the floating platters behind her. "They've got pobyd magic on them, so they'll be fine."

He thumbed at a door near the end of the bar that Lillie hadn't noticed before. She walked through and found a room already filled with tables and chairs, as well as a lectern. She plucked each of the platters out of the air and placed them on the buffets against the wall, adjusting them so the prettiest pastries were in the front. Then, satisfied, she turned to leave.

"I'll be back later," Lillie said with a wave.

"I'm sure I don't care."

~

Lillie began her trek to Honeygold Farms, stopping only for a moment at Greeley's shop to pick up a tincture that could speed up healing.

"Bones are tricky things," he said, echoing what Reginald had told her. "But this should help with the pain and set the bone right."

With the tincture safely tucked away in her pocket, Lillie continued up the hill toward the Silverkeep town square. She hadn't been back this way since the mushrooms took residence in a few shops and was pleased to see everything was back as it had been. Reginald had done a good job of repairing all Ned had destroyed, and it was hard to tell there'd been any mushrooms at all.

She hurried on but couldn't help sending a longing glance toward Globe Café. Too late she realized she should've written back to Julian and dropped the response on his doorstep. But it was still the middle of the afternoon, and since she was doing her level best to avoid being seen cavorting with any of the Globes, it was probably for the best.

The incline leveled out, and soon Lillie was on a dirt road flanked with rolling green fields. It was hard to remember, being so far down in the town, that there were verdant hills beyond the bustling city, and one could get lost in the farmlands.

She arrived at the pretty house and rapped on the door, stepping back and waiting. There was a loud thumping inside, and a moment later, the door opened to reveal Kristin's surprised face. She was leaning on a pair of crutches, and her leg had been covered in plaster to hold it in a straight position.

"Lillie, goodness, what are you doing here?" Kristin asked, surprise lighting her eyes.

"I heard about your accident," Lillie said. "Are you all right?"

"Been better, but I'm surviving." Kristin smiled. "Come on in."

"Your sister-in-law isn't around, is she?" Lillie asked. "I already got an earful from Esmerelda."

"No, she's in the dairy, and should be for the rest of the day." Kristin's brow furrowed. "What did

Essi say to you?"

"Well, you're going to be getting a lecture," Lillie said. "And we're no longer allowed to barter."

Kristin made a dismissive sound. "You know, we've been making *more* money since I started selling the butter, but they never listen to anything I say. They're so shortsighted, you know?" She adjusted her stance on the crutches. "I hope she at least dropped off your milk and eggs this morning."

"She did not," Lillie said. "And told me she was no longer going to deliver them, either."

"That little..." Kristin hobbled over to the floral-print couch, gratefully accepting Lillie's help to settle down onto the cushions. "I'll talk to her about it, but I fear she's pretty set in her ways. And with this bum leg, I'm pretty much confined to the couch until it heals in six weeks."

"Goodness, six weeks?" Lillie sighed. "That's awful. I asked Reginald about it, but he said bones are too complex."

"And I think Essi would kick me out if I let a mage in the house," Kristin said with a chuckle. "So I'm stuck here. Reading and wasting away."

It was clear from the stacks of books, cups, and dirty plates, not to mention the pillow and blanket, that Kristin wasn't going very far.

Lillie took the seat opposite her, perched on the edge of the cushions. "So what in the world happened? I heard something about a roof?"

"Just silly, that's all," Kristin said. "We had a leak yesterday, and I thought I might get up there and fix it. Ended up slipping and, well, landed wrong." She shook her head, poking at the plaster around her leg. "Had to get a doc in from Bell's Keep to plaster it all up."

"Oh, that reminds me," Lillie said, reaching into her pocket. "Tincture from the Slooses. Greeley says this should help with the pain and expedite the healing."

"Aw, Lillie, you shouldn't have," Kristin said, popping off the cork and downing it. "Just don't mention it to my sister."

"I wouldn't dare," Lillie said. "I'm already on thin ice being here."

Kristin snorted as she adjusted a pillow behind her back. "They're just… I mean, I don't know. They're more ornery than usual. We've been having some money troubles—and now I'm out of commission, which is making it doubly hard." She sighed. "I told Essi I could sit at the booth with this leg, but she told me to stay home and rest. But that means Charla's here by herself, tending to the cows *and* milking them *and* getting everything bottled up. We don't have the money to hire anyone—not even temporarily."

"I can understand that," Lillie said. "If there's

anything I can do..."

"This tincture is working pretty well." Kristin sighed as her eyelids drooped. "Making me sleepy, though. Is that a side effect?"

"I'm not sure," Lillie said, standing to help tuck Kristin in. "But let's say yes."

Kristin nestled back into the pillows and was asleep before Lillie finished covering her leg. Lillie patted her friend's head then began gathering plates and dishes, taking them to the kitchen and giving them a wash. Then she found a bit of freshly baked bread in the pantry, along with some cheese and dried meat, and made Kristin a sandwich.

"Now listen," Lillie whispered to the food. "I know you're already made and baked, but if you've got a mind to hear me, please make yourself extra nutritious and delicious for my dear friend. She's in a bad way, and she needs all the help she can get for her leg to heal correctly."

The sandwich gave no sign that it had heard her, but Lillie placed it, along with a fresh cup of water, on the table beside Kristin's snoozing form. Then she tidied up the crumbs and restacked the books, before deciding she'd done enough.

"You heal quickly," Lillie whispered, patting Kristin on her plaster cast. "I'll be by to check on you when I can."

"What are you doing here?" An angry voice

echoed from the doorway.

Lillie spun to find Esmerelda's wife Charla standing in the doorway. She looked absolutely caked in mud, her pale cheeks flushed with heat, and her hair plastered to her forehead.

"I was checking on my friend," Lillie said. "And tidying up a bit—"

"I saw you do magic on that bread," Charla snapped. "It's going in the trash."

"That's silly," Lillie said. "My magic doesn't even work that well on things that are already baked—"

"Nonetheless, we don't like any sort of magic in this house. Now, if you don't leave, I'm going to call the sheriff. I know she hates you—"

"Hate is a strong word," Lillie muttered. "But I do need to be getting back. Please tell Kristin—"

Charla glared at her.

"On second thought, don't tell her anything," Lillie said, making a beeline toward the door and barely breaking her stride until she was safely back in Silverkeep.

Lillie stopped at her apartment long enough to freshen up and do something with her wild blonde curls, before her neighbor Ursil Koven was knocking at her door, ready to escort her to the Fisherfolk Council meeting. He wore an unusually spiffy tunic, with his windswept hair slicked back with grease, and his shoes looked to be recently shined.

"Don't you look lovely?" Lillie said, closing the door behind her after making sure she had Wineke's pamphlets in hand.

"Gotta put our best foot forward, you know," Ursil said. "Nik's already there, saving our seats and presumably chatting away with the McTavishes. Gotta make them happy, else we might end up losing our meal ticket."

Lillie patted him on the arm. "I don't think you two have anything to worry about. Orxan and Jan have told me they're eager to keep Nikola bringing in the fish."

"Yeah, it's not them I'm worried about," Ursil said with a grimace.

"What do you mean?" Lillie said with a frown.

"I don't think they're the only ones running this year," he said. "But we'll have to see when we get there. I'm hoping it's a rumor. Already too much change in town." He smirked. "I saw you going at it with Esmerelda Honeygold this afternoon. Did you find out where Kristin is?"

Lillie told him about Kristin's leg, and he muttered something unsavory under his breath. "She barely looked in my direction today. Surprised she sold *anything* with that attitude. She's really not going to be bringing you milk and eggs in the morning?"

"Guess not," Lillie said, not looking forward to the extra trips. "But what can you do? At least Kristin drank that tincture from the Slooses before her sister-in-law came in."

The Sad Hill Pub was bustling at this hour, with the magical folks who'd moved back to town taking up most of the tables instead of the sailors and fisherfolk. Lillie didn't suppose the bartender minded his new clientele, as long as his dining room was busy, but she'd always gotten the sense he was as big a fan of the magical set as Esmerelda Honeygold. The sailors from the wharf were still around, though they'd been relegated to the bar and some of the tables in the back.

Still, Clifton gave Ursil a begrudging nod as the fishmonger led Lillie to the room in the back, which had been decorated with light blue paper decorations and seemed much more festive. Lillie parted ways with Ursil, who went to find his bride, and sidled up to the pastries assembled on the table, none of which had been touched yet. There was also a large bowl filled with red punch, along with stacked cups that hadn't been used.

She'd encouraged them to stay fresh before she'd left, but she whispered a few more words to the cookies.

"More of your mind control?"

Lillie blanched and straightened, facing Jarvis Collin, who wore a look of disgust.

"I don't do mind control," Lillie replied sweetly. "Merely making sure my product remains as delicious as ever."

He snorted, coming to stand at the table. "I still say those things are dangerous. I ain't eating them."

"Good for you," Lillie muttered, turning back to her pastries and purposefully ignoring Jarvis. He'd never been nice to her, though he seemed to tolerate Ursil, whose booth was next to his. Lillie got the impression he disliked all magical people and things, as he harbored jealousy and suspicion about Nikola's fishing abilities.

Luckily, Jarvis didn't stick around long, and was replaced by a smiling Jan McTavish. "Lillie, good to see you. These look amazing."

"I'm glad to hear it," she said. "Nobody's taken any yet." She pointed to the lemon tartlets. "I made those especially for you."

"Oh, did you?" Jan plucked up one of the tartlets and took a bite. "As usual, Lillie, the most delicious things in the world."

"Well, not the most delicious," Lillie muttered with a knowing wink. "But I'm glad you enjoy them."

Jan seemed to break the ice for the rest of the fisherfolk, who descended on the table, and within minutes, there was nary a crumb remaining. Every single person in the room had a cup of punch and a pastry—except Jarvis, of course, who sat scowling at the entire room.

"Oh, ignore him," Hipolita Tokely, one of the fisherfolk, said. "I think he knows he's not getting a slip again, and it's made him cranky."

Keegan Curtis took a large bite of the lemon tartlet. "You know, I don't get down to the bakery as much as I should. These are delightful. Do you take custom orders?"

"Of course I do," Lillie said with a bright smile. "If there's any sweet you'd like me to put on my list, I'm always taking requests."

"Oh, I don't have anything in particular. Give me a good chocolate chip cookie, and I'm content," Keegan said.

"I do make a batch or two of those every day," Lillie said. "They're my bestsellers."

"And how." Glen Jacob, one-half of the twin fisherfolk who were some of Lillie's best customers, joined the conversation. "I think I buy about six a day, don't I?"

"Between you and your brother, yes," Lillie said. "Not to mention the standing muffin order with Evangeline."

"Ah, the best part of my morning," Glen said, covering his heart with a satisfied smile. "What were those ones you made the other day?"

"Cinnamon crumble," Lillie said. "Kind of a cross between a coffee cake and a muffin."

"Make those again," Glen said with an emphatic nod.

"Oh, that does sound good," Hipolita said. "I do love cinnamon."

"I made some cinnamon chip scones this morning," Lillie said. "They've got little pockets of sweet and spicy in them. Some of my favorites."

"You know, I think you and Julian Globe should team up," Keegan said. "When I lived up north, I used to get these little biscotti with a coffee—have you heard of those? They bake 'em in a big log, cut them up into smaller cookies, and bake 'em again so they're nice and crunchy. Perfect for dunking in coffee."

"Interesting," Lillie said, willing her cheeks to remain unflushed at the mention of Julian. "I'll look into those. They sound delicious."

And perhaps something Lillie could put in her letter back to Julian. On the long walk back from Kristin's, she'd already started mentally penning her response and scheming how she could get it to him without being seen. Despite knowing what was at stake if Mr. Globe found out, Lillie couldn't help but feel a little thrill at the prospect of sneaking around behind his back—even if it was in written form.

Lillie meandered around the room, talking with the other Jacob twin and his wife Evangeline, as well as some of the merchants who'd come to offer their opinion about the setup. Lillie's sugar merchant Eduardo was there, as was the grandson of Ewing Dupont, who sold her the bulk of her produce.

She'd seen more of Jarod than Ewing lately, and the way Jarod talked about his plans gave Lillie the clear impression he was about to take over.

"Gramps is so old, you know?" the younger Dupont said. "But I think he'll still want to be the one handling all the growing and that sort of thing. You can't get him away from that."

"You said it," Eduardo agreed. "It'll be strange not to see him at your booth, but time marches on, I suppose. I'm glad Kemp Abora is running for mayor. We've seen enough change recently."

Lillie forced a smile, unsure if this was the right time to mention Wineke, but the conversation quickly moved on to something else, and Lillie couldn't find the right segue to talk about her apothecary friend, like she'd promised. Before she could find one, Jan McTavish pulled her aside for a private conversation.

"How's it going?" they asked. "Does it seem like everyone's happy with the pastries?"

Lillie shrugged. "I can't imagine they wouldn't be. Why? What's wrong?"

"I got confirmation that this *isn't* going to be business as usual tonight," Jan said, nodding to the door.

A woman with pale skin, dark brown hair, and eagle-like eyes swept into the room. Lillie got the distinct impression she was *always* busy, and as her heeled shoes clacked on the wooden floor, they set her teeth on edge. The newcomer regarded the room as if it were filled with filth before spotting Jarvis and marching over to him.

"Who's that?" Lillie asked.

"Kathryn Harkness," Jan replied.

"Wait, that's Mr. Globe's—I mean, Clancy Cast's mayoral campaign manager, isn't it?" Lillie said. "What's she doing here? I thought the mayor's conference wasn't for another few days."

"She's not here for the mayor," Jan said. "She's working for Jarvis. He's thrown his hat in the ring for Fisherfolk Council."

Lillie couldn't believe that—except that Kathryn had walked right up to the fisherfolk and pulled him aside, shoving a stack of papers into his hand and pointing at them emphatically.

"That's odd," Lillie said. "Mr. Globe's paying her to manage two campaigns?"

"Not confirmed, but that's what Orxan and I suspect," Jan said. "She's been sniffing around the fisherfolk, trying to get the lay of the land. We'd thought it was for Clancy, but..."

Jarvis was arguing with her about something, and she gave him a look so severe he wilted.

"Clearly, she's helping both campaigns," Lillie finished. "So Mr. Globe doesn't want you two in charge either, does he?"

Jan sighed. "I can't imagine it's a coincidence—or that Jarvis has enough money to pay for her himself. All he wants is to give himself a slip at the dock, so if Mr. Globe's offering to put him in charge, he'll do whatever it takes."

"I don't think... A campaign manager isn't going to change much," Lillie said, thinking of her earlier conversations about the mayoral race. "These folks know you, and they know you've always done right by them."

At that precise moment, Kathryn's gaze met Lillie's, and her red lips quirked up in a knowing smile.

"Here we go," Lillie muttered, as the other woman marched over.

"You must be the infamous Lillie Dean," Kathryn said, holding out her hand and introducing herself. "So good to meet you."

"Likewise," Lillie said, getting a decidedly unsettling feeling from her—and not loving that Mr. Globe's campaign manager knew about her already. But she would be kind first and figure out the rest later. "What brings you to our small town?"

"What else? Money." She laughed and quickly brushed a strand of hair from her forehead with a single finger. "That, and Julian Globe and I have a little history, so I was happy to see *his* handsome face again."

Lillie's heart stumbled over itself. "I'm...sorry?"

"Yes, Julian and I go way back. Took some business classes together in Sheepsburg. One thing led to another, until we were making out in the back of the local tavern." She laughed again, using that same finger to adjust her perfectly shaped hair. "He's quite a romantic. Excellent kisser. Can't complain about that."

It took every ounce of Lillie's self-control not to rip that brown lock of hair out of Kathryn's head. "You don't say."

"I swear, I think Audo invited me here just to turn his head." She laughed again, as if Lillie's love life were a hilarious joke. "I hear he's been sweet on another baker. I can only assume that's you, right?"

"No," Lillie forced herself to say, even though Jan's curious gaze was on her. "Julian and I are colleagues. He's got his bakery, and I have mine. We help each other out professionally. But otherwise, there's nothing to talk about."

"Yes, well, from what I hear, yours is doing better than his, so I'm sure Audo's going to make sure that changes soon, hm?" She turned to Jan, who'd been standing there silently. "Hello there. I don't think we've met. You're one of the McIntoshes, right?"

"McTavishes," Jan said.

"Yeah, it doesn't matter." Kathryn turned

toward the group with a sharklike smile. "Well, shall we get this show on the road? I've got to get back up to that butcher and quiz him on his policy talking points. You know, I don't think Audo is paying me enough for all this, but..." She shrugged. "What can you do?"

With that, she bustled away toward the table where Jarvis was sitting, leaving Lillie and Jan to stare wordlessly after her.

"Well, she is certainly...something," Jan said, after a moment. "But she's right. It's about time for the discussions to start."

Lillie, who was fighting the urge to march right up to Globe Café and have words with Julian, instead plopped down next to Ursil and Nikola.

"Who's that fancy gal?" Ursil asked.

"The new campaign manager," Lillie said. "For Jarvis *and* Clancy Cast for mayor. Both paid for by Mr. Globe, so I assume."

"That scoundrel," Ursil said. "You know, one of these days, he's gonna learn to stop meddling in other people's affairs."

Lillie only nodded vaguely as Orxan and Jan took to the lectern to open the meeting. She didn't bother to listen to what they were saying, as it didn't really pertain to her. Instead, she kept stealing glances at Kathryn. What in the world could Julian possibly see in her?

Lillie supposed she was pretty. Her brown hair was slick and smooth, and her lips an immaculate shade of red. Meanwhile, Lillie's wild blonde curls were difficult to tame and usually ended up frizzing out of a messy bun atop her head. She also never wore any sort of makeup and her nails were far too short and stubby—a hazard of working with food all day. And her clothes, well, those were the boring sort of shirts and skirts, and *also* fell victim to working with flour, sugar, and chocolate.

Insecurity was a new feeling for Lillie, and she didn't like it.

But her thoughts were interrupted when she realized there was an argument happening.

"The McTavishes have done us no favors recently, have they?" Jarvis was saying. He stood at his table, Kathryn quickly writing down notes and passing them over. "Everybody's dock fees are going up, and they're doing *nothing* about it."

"If you think we haven't been pressing Audo Globe to lower them, you're dreaming," Orxan said with a scowl. "That man controls everything in this town. And if you try to go against him—"

"We don't need to go against him," Jarvis cut him off. "I say we get him to agree to the same deal we had before. But I don't think you two can make that bargain anymore, can you?"

The room broke into quiet murmurs. Kathryn

looked smug. Jarvis seemed shocked that his argument worked. And the McTavishes were at a loss for words.

"Are you suggesting you can do better?" Jan sputtered after a moment.

"I'm pretty sure I can."

"Didn't you say that woman works for Mr. Globe?" Ursil whispered to Lillie.

She nodded, curious. Jarvis seemed the sort lacking in connections. But perhaps this was Mr. Globe's plan all along—raise the dock fees to unsustainable levels, then offer his choice as an alternative to bring them back down.

She glanced at the McTavishes, who were starting to look a little sweaty. And green.

In fact, everyone in the room had a decidedly green tint—including Ursil and Nikola.

"Are you all right?" Lillie whispered to Ursil as he covered his mouth and cleared his throat.

"Something's not sitting right with me," Ursil said, swallowing hard. "I'm sure it's—"

Jan McTavish hiccupped—and a sprinkle of pink dust flew from under their shirt. They jumped up with a gasp and ran from the room. Orxan, covering his mouth and looking quite sick, was right behind them.

Then, in a mad dash that saw overturned chairs and thunderous foot stomps, the rest of the room followed, leaving only Lillie, Jarvis, and Kathryn.

"Well, isn't that interesting?" Kathryn muttered. "Must've been something in the punch, eh?"

Needless to say, the scene outside the Sad Hill Pub was most unpleasant.

Lillie did her best to forget the particular details as she tucked herself into bed, instead trying to piece together what had happened. Maybe Clifton had mixed the wrong ingredients together to make the punch. Or, more insidiously, someone had *added* something to the punch to create an issue for the McTavishes. After all, it was their event. And it was a little too coincidental that Jarvis hadn't gotten sick —nor did it seem like happenstance that Kathryn had mentioned the punch offhand.

*Kathryn.* Lillie stared at the dark ceiling, glaring at an imagined visage of the campaign manager. She wasn't one to jump to conclusions, of course. But Kathryn seemed the sort to do whatever it took to win, and Lillie didn't like her at all.

Which had absolutely nothing to do with the fact that she and Julian had dated.

Lillie slept fitfully, too racked with unease to really find rest. In the morning, she went downstairs, intending to start the morning's bakes, only to remember that she'd used up all her milk and egg and wouldn't be getting a morning delivery from Esmerelda.

"Suppose we'll have to make do," Lillie muttered. "And get started later."

Thankfully, she still had leftovers from yesterday morning's bake, though they'd be on the cusp of what she felt comfortable selling. When the clock struck seven, Lillie headed down to the wharf market, only to find it deader than expected. All the booths were empty and all the boats were still in their slips. Then again, most everyone had been at the Fisherfolk Council the night before, and most everyone had been *less* than hale at the end of it. Lillie hadn't even considered they might still be ill.

As she drew closer, there was one person at her post—Esmerelda Honeygold, who glowered at Lillie as she approached. "I hear you were in my home yesterday," she said, by way of introduction.

"I was checking on my dear friend," Lillie replied. "And I'm here to pick up the day's milk and eggs."

"I don't suppose you know what's going on, do you?" Esmerelda asked. "Where is everybody? Did I miss some kind of announcement about the market being closed today?"

"Oh, that's right, you weren't at the Fisherfolk Council meeting last night," Lillie said. "Seems like someone spiked the punch and got everyone sick."

Esmerelda frowned. "What? Who'd do that?"

*Kathryn.* "No idea." Lillie tilted her head. "Why weren't you there? You were invited, weren't you?"

"Are you joking?" she scoffed. "As if we have time to fritter away at a *meeting* when our farm is short on labor. I was in the barn with Charla, milking the cows. Churning butter. Packing the wagon so I could try to make a living." She snorted, looking around. "Not as if anyone's buying at the moment. Lotta work wasted."

"You know, the deal is still on the table if you'd like me to churn the butter to sell," Lillie said gently.

Esmerelda glared at her. "I'm not selling *anything* with a lick of magic in it."

"Suit yourself." Lillie shrugged and returned to the bakery, counting the minutes until Kristin was back at her post.

Lillie stashed the supplies in the back to save. With no one at the wharf, that meant her bakery's business would be down, too. Instead of her usual fare of cookies and cupcakes, she instead started several batches of bread. Even with her pobyd encouragement, they'd take a few hours to be ready, but at least she'd have something to sell that might tempt a customer.

She needn't have worried. By the time her first customer—Wineke—came in, the bread had already risen, been shaped, risen again, and baked, and it was now cool and ready to be sliced.

"What in the world is going on out there?" Wineke asked. "And why have we gotten about twenty orders for anti-nausea tinctures since we've opened?"

"Well, it seems someone wanted to cause trouble at the Fisherfolk Council last night," Lillie said. "I'm pretty sure someone put something in the punch."

"Did you get sick?" Wineke asked then tapped her finger against her chin. "Can pobyds get food poisoning?"

"My magic usually lets me know before I ingest anything rancid," Lillie said. "Either by smell or by first taste—sometimes by touch, even. I didn't have any of the punch, though."

"Ooh, another mystery afoot?" Wineke said with an excited grin. "Perhaps someone out to sabotage the Fisherfolk Council?"

"That's my guess," Lillie said. "Everyone but Jarvis Collin and his new campaign manager got sick."

"He's got one of those, too?" Wineke scowled. "Maybe I should've gotten one. Do you want to do it?"

"No, thanks," Lillie said. "I'm no good at politics. Besides that, the same woman is managing both Jarvis's and Clancy's campaigns."

"Really? And paid for by Mr. Globe?" She bit her lip. "Then everyone got poisoned but them. Gosh, that's concerning, isn't it?"

"In more ways than one," Lillie said, trying not to remember how Kathryn had *so casually* mentioned what a good kisser Julian was. "I'm sure… Well, I don't think it was nothing, but I'm sure the McTavishes would tell Juno if they thought anything was amiss."

"Would she do anything about it?" Wineke said. "You're the resident mystery solver around town these days. I hear you're the one who figured out Tom's brother was behind the mushroom attacks. I mean, we probably should've guessed. Tom wouldn't hurt a fly, but his brother was a nasty piece of work."

"Mm." Lillie was grateful everyone believed Tom oblivious to his brother's evil deeds.

"Was there anything left of the punch?" Wineke asked.

Lillie shook her head. "No. Why?"

"Darn," Wineke said. "Greeley could've run some tests on it. He likes a good challenge, and discerning what poison has made everyone sick would certainly be tricky."

"I need to go back to the Sad Hill to collect my platters anyway," Lillie said. "I can ask Clifton if there was any left, but I doubt it."

"You left your platters?" Wineke asked.

"Well, if you were there, you wouldn't have blamed me. It was an awful, *awful* scene, and it was all I could do to get Ursil and Nikola back home." She waved Wineke off. "You don't want to know the details."

"Did you talk to them about me?" Wineke asked with a hopeful smile.

In her heart, Lillie knew she could've done better but didn't want to disappoint her friend. "There's another event happening tomorrow night. Surely you're invited to that one, right?"

She nodded. "Yeah. I've still got to prepare my speech. I'm so nervous about all of it. I keep tripping over my words."

"You're going to do great," Lillie said. "You've

already got Ursil and Nikola on your side. And Jeremias, for sure. The others...well, I'm not sure they're reachable. But I bet you the McTavishes would love to chat with you..." She winced. "When they're feeling better."

Lillie was unfortunately vindicated in her decision to hold off on baking anything else as the morning wore on. Other than Wineke, only Haruko and Edwina Featherswift came for a sweet treat. She spotted a few green-faced fisherfolk stumbling into Greeley's apothecary, but for the most part, everyone avoided the bakery.

"I say, I should've come with you," Rey said when he came out for his morning pastry—a double chocolate chip cookie that was almost too stale to serve. "I could've kept an eye on things—found out if someone slipped something into the punch."

"I can't believe someone would do that to their friends intentionally," Lillie said. "How was the Silverkeep Inn last night? Abuzz with election talk?"

"And how. I hear Clancy's doing his first rally tonight at the Silverkeep Inn. Hopefully, he'll avoid any punch-related poisonings." Rey looked down at the cookie suspiciously. "How sure are you that it was the punch? Should I be concerned about my sensitive stomach?"

"Wineke had a muffin earlier and hasn't

complained," Lillie said. "I think you're safe."

"But it could've been someone out to cause trouble for *you*, Lillie," Rey said, taking a large bite of his cookie. "You do have a few enemies."

"Don't I know it," Lillie said, thinking of Kathryn's comment about Mr. Globe wanting to run her out of town. "But I think it was the punch. It seems much easier to tip a vial of something into a large liquid than to sprinkle it over three platters." She glanced around, as if worried her words would echo. "Then again, I did leave my pastries unattended for a few hours."

"Hm." Rey rubbed his whiskers. "Why'd you do that?"

"Well, because I didn't think anyone would do anything to them!" Lillie said with a frown. "Besides that, I didn't want to risk being late. I was going to visit Kristin, and you know she can talk sometimes..."

"True, true. But not as bad as Penelope Bigears." He shuddered. "She *never* knows when to shut up."

Lillie chuckled. "Between you and me, I do hope it's the punch. My business is already suffering enough today without rumors starting that my pastries are poisoned."

"I don't think you have anything to worry about. The people of Silverkeep know that Pobyd Perfections Bakery is the pinnacle of quality and fresh ingredients," Rey said, puffing out his chest. "I daresay as the bakery assistant—"

"You?" Lillie scoffed. "When was the last time you *ever* helped bake anything?"

"I'm here for moral support!" Rey said with a scowl.

Lillie laughed. "Whatever you say, Rey."

~

With nearly the entire wharf market out sick, Lillie had a very quiet day. She paced the bakery, testing her goods three and four times to make sure. She didn't sense anything terribly off about them, and, of course, she'd sold to several folks and none had reported ill effects.

But that didn't mean someone hadn't sabotaged her last night.

She couldn't help but think about those hours her goods had been left unattended. Well, not completely unattended. Clifton had been there, supposedly. Did he have some vendetta against her she didn't know about?

Of course, if Mr. Globe had put him up to it, he wouldn't need a grudge. Kathryn, too, could've popped in early under the guise of setting up for the event. Perhaps even Ned, Tom's brother, had somehow broken out of the wizard prison and was back to take revenge, but considering Tom was still very human, Lillie dismissed that idea as too far-fetched.

As the afternoon wore on, Lillie considered closing for the day and retrieving her platters from the Sad Hill, when the McTavishes lumbered by her window and walked inside.

"Jan, Orxan, how are you feeling?" Lillie asked.

"Awful," Jan said, pressing their handkerchief to their lips and swallowing hard as they sank into a nearby chair. "I've never been this sick in my life."

"I'm so sorry," Lillie said.

"You seem to have come out all right," Orxan said.

"I didn't drink any of the punch," Lillie said with a smile. "Thankfully."

"You think it was the punch, then?" Jan asked. "We're racking our brains, trying to figure out what it could've been."

"And why they might've done it," Orxan said gravely. "Since we didn't get to have our chat last night, we're hoping to redo it tomorrow, combining it with the mayoral discussion. And, erm..." He frowned. "Considering what happened at the first meeting, we're going to have to cancel our pastry order."

A noise of protest erupted from Lillie before she could stop it. "You don't think it was me, do you?"

"Of course not," Jan said, glancing at the pastry case and shaking their head. "But I still think it's going to be a few days before I can eat another lemon tartlet without feeling sick."

"Hang on," Lillie said. "I've got just the thing."

She pulled one of the whole loaves from the back and sliced it in half, before bringing it out with the refund for the second night of pastries.

"Thanks." Jan burped, and a spark of pink fairy dust came flying from underneath their shirt.

Lillie gasped and covered her mouth, glancing at Orxan nervously. The same thing had happened the night before, but Lillie had hoped for Jan's sake no one had noticed. Yet Jan's partner pulled out a handkerchief and wiped it up as if this weren't the first fairy dust he'd swept up today.

"Erm..." Lillie cleared her throat. "That's..."

"Been happening all morning," Jan said darkly. "I wasn't just sick last night, either. My wings made an appearance. And no matter how much iron dust I took, they wouldn't go away. I'm lucky I got home before they popped out." They glanced at Orxan. "Unfortunately, couldn't hide them from everyone."

"I knew, sweetheart," Orxan said with a shake of his head. "I mean, I didn't know how big they actually were, but I've seen fairy dust around the apartment. Was waiting for you to be comfortable enough to tell me."

Lillie smiled. One very small silver lining. Jan had been so worried about sharing their secret with their partner, even though Lillie had been sure it wouldn't be a big deal.

"Thank goodness no one else noticed anything," Jan said.

"Well, I'm glad everything's out in the open now, at least between you two," she said. "But that does make for an interesting new wrinkle."

"Interesting? Suspicious is more like it," Jan said darkly. "I know we're on good terms, but the rest of the fisherfolk veer on the side of anti-magic. If they found out I had pink wings and fairy dust, they might vote against me out of spite."

"You think that was the intent?" Lillie asked.

"Certainly seems that way," Orxan said.

"Did Clifton tell you anything?" Lillie asked.

"That's actually why we've come to talk with you," Jan said. "You've gotten a bit of a reputation for fixing stuff in town. Do you think you could…I don't know, sniff around a bit?"

"Why don't you ask Sheriff Juno to look into it?"

"Because I got a feeling Mr. Globe might be the actual culprit," Orxan said. "We've lost his favor, and the fact that Jarvis Collin suddenly decided to throw his hat in the ring? Suspicious."

"What do you mean lost his favor?" Lillie asked.

"Well, with all the queen- and kingside folks changing things, we thought we might have some recourse against him," Orxan said. "His purchase of the wharf wasn't exactly done in the most legal of ways, if you catch my drift. We'd hoped there might be a loophole, that it's not quite as all-encompassing as he's made it out to be. He caught wind that we were sniffing around, and now Jarvis is running for council."

"What would change if Mr. Globe didn't own the wharf?" Lillie asked.

"Well, we wouldn't overcharge the fisherfolk for their dock fees, that's for sure," Jan said. "And we might be able to wrest a few of the big slips away from him and create some room for all the fisherfolk who want one."

"And he wouldn't like that." It wasn't a question. Mr. Globe was a man who always sought the best deal for himself, usually at the expense of everyone else. Losing not only the dock fees but also one of his slips would surely encourage the man to find someone else to back.

"I can't promise anything," Lillie said, after a moment, "But I'll head up to the Sad Hill Pub to sniff around—and ask the fisherfolk what they saw last night. Maybe Greeley has some deliveries he needs me to make."

"That would be great," Orxan said, grimacing. "We'd go, but we're not in a state to walk around right now."

"I can see that," Lillie said. "Go home and rest. I'll let you know if I find anything." She paused. "But first, stop next door and let Greeley give you a tincture or two."

"I can't take anything magical," Jan said, but Orxan put his hand on their shoulder.

"Yes, you can. No need to hide anything from me anymore, you know." He squeezed.

Jan smiled, relief shining in their eyes. "Well, if you insist."

Lillie sighed, happy *some* good had come from all this, but disappointed that yet again, the problems of Silverkeep had fallen on her shoulders.

Once the McTavishes had left, Lillie headed straight to the Sad Hill Pub to check things out. She wasn't very optimistic she'd find any lingering evidence—everything had been consumed well before the illnesses began—but she owed it to the McTavishes to start there, anyway. Perhaps Clifton had seen something.

The wharf market was still as empty as Lillie's bakery—even Esmerelda had finally left her post—and Lillie wasn't even sure Clifton would be there so early in the afternoon. Thankfully, the door was open, and said bartender was already wiping down tables and glasses.

"Eh? What do you want?" he said when Lillie walked in the door. "Returning to the scene of the crime?"

"Excuse me?" Lillie's eyes narrowed.

"Ever'one ate one of your pastries, didn't they?"

"It was *the punch*," Lillie said, putting her hands on her hips. "And even if it was my pastries, it certainly didn't originate in my kitchen. Clearly, someone's out to cause trouble. And they succeeded." She put her hands on her hips. "Do you still have my platters?"

He thumbed toward the back room, and Lillie quickly went to retrieve them. He'd already cleaned and dried them (which was nice of him), but she was a tad disappointed. Not that she wanted it to have originated in her food, but a crumb or two would've been helpful to give to Greeley.

She returned to the front room where Clifton was still wiping down glasses. "If that'll be all—"

"No," Lillie said, walking up to the bar and placing the platters down as she sat across from him. "I want to know everything that happened last night. The full schedule of events that preceded everyone getting sick. Who was first to arrive? Who was left alone in the room with the pastries—?"

He chuckled. "Are you the new sheriff in town?"

"No, but..." Lillie breathed through her news.

"The McTavishes asked me to look into what happened. They feel I might have better luck than Juno."

"Is that so?" He didn't look impressed. "I thought Jan and Orxan were smarter than that. Why'd they hire the person responsible for it?"

"Yesterday," Lillie continued, undeterred, "I dropped the pastries off mid-afternoon. Who was the first person in that room after me?"

"Couldn't tell you," he said. "And no, I'm not tryin' to protect anybody or keep secrets. I made the punch after you walked out the door and left it in there. The first round of diners showed up around four, then it's steady business until closing time. I didn't pay attention to who was comin' and goin', except, of course, Jarvis's campaign manager."

Lillie tried to keep a straight face and failed. "Oh? Why her?"

"She's high maintenance." He shook his head. "I'm not in the habit of waiting hand and foot on people. She kept askin' for a different kinda water—one that, she said, wasn't filled with dirt. I told 'er I have the same water I give everyone, and if she wanted something diff'rent she could find it elsewhere. But she kept snappin' her fingers and orderin' me to fetch her different water."

"Did you?" Lillie asked with a smile.

He huffed. "No. Eventually, she gave up on

water and started demandin' a 'higher quality alcohol.' I'm glad I had a bottle of sommin' in the back that suited her tastes, or I might've canceled the whole council meetin' and gone home for the night."

"I bet." Lillie felt a little warmer toward the bartender. "Well, thanks for the information. I wish there was something leftover from what we ate and drank last night. Greeley said he could test it."

He stopped cleaning the glass. "What d'ya mean test?"

"Greeley's an apothecary," Lillie said. "A good one, unlike others in town. He could potentially figure out what caused everyone to get sick if we had a sample of it."

Clifton put down the glass and walked into the back room. A moment later, he came out with a glass of red punch.

Lillie's mouth fell open. "Is that—?"

"Jan brought some over to me before everythin' got started," he said. "I didn't get a chance to drink it—too busy—but when everyone started, well, you know, I *really* didn't want to drink it. Forgot about it until now." He picked up the glass. "If you wanna take that to your apothecary, I'm sure he could do somethin' with it. But I still think it was the pastries."

"Why do you say that?" Lillie asked.

"Because my punch ain't got no poison in it. And I'll thank you to quit spreadin' rumors about my business until you know otherwise."

"*If* it was poisoned," Lillie said gently, "there's a good chance someone added it later. I can't imagine someone who caters to the fisherfolk on a regular basis would want to hurt them."

"Too right." He snorted and picked up another glass. "Well? That's all I got to share at the moment. So unless you want to pick up a broom and start cleanin', I suggest you get to gettin'."

~

"Oh, my," Greeley said, considering the red liquid as if it were volatile and explosive. "What a stroke of good luck, eh?"

"Hopefully," Lillie said. "Wineke said you could test it, right?"

"For sure," Fawn squeaked from the counter. "We'll find the source, no problem."

"Well, let's not count our chickens before we know what we're dealing with," Greeley said, sniffing it. "I can't immediately tell anything offensive. But a lot of poisons are colorless and tasteless—that's what makes them so dangerous."

"You do think it was poison?" Lillie asked.

"I mean, the fact that everyone is *still* sick? Yes." Greeley nodded toward the front door. "This whole day, all we've sold are anti-nausea tinctures—and poor Glen Jacob had to come back for another one because he couldn't keep the first vial down."

"Poor dear." Lillie covered her mouth.

"From what he described to me, it's pretty consistent with poison—especially since the onset was so sudden," Greeley said, looking at the juice in the light. "We'll run some tests for the usual suspects, which might help me make a better tincture, too. I did add a little antivenom into the latest batch, and that seemed to help Nikola and Ursil."

"You've been giving them tinctures?" Lillie asked. Nikola's nymph heritage was still a secret, so Lillie didn't want to ask outright if she'd asked for anything to hide her magic. "Who else has gotten one?"

He listed off nearly the entire Fisherfolk Council. "I think a good number of them would've rather gone to see Zena, but they didn't want to make the trek up the hill."

Lillie chewed her lip, thinking of what the McTavishes had shared with her. "Is it nausea? No one's complained of anything else?"

"Not particularly," Greeley said with a frown. "Why?"

"I've heard from a few people that there was another symptom," Lillie said. "Apparently, it's making latent or small bits of magic appear in people who otherwise didn't have any."

"Oh." Greeley's brows knitted together. "Now that is interesting. A concoction that makes nonmagical people sick *and* encourages magic to present itself?" He rubbed his chin. "Fawn?"

"That could be any number of poisons," she said, thoughtfully. "But it does narrow the list from thousands to hundreds, at least."

Greeley beamed. "Ah, that is good news!"

Lillie had to hide a smile. Wineke had said Greeley was hoping for a challenge, and clearly, she'd been right to assume this was a good one for him.

More than that, Lillie was grateful she could trust them. Both Greeley and Fawn had made bad decisions that had nearly resulted in calamity, but thankfully, came to their senses before any major damage had been done. Lillie had kept their secrets, and they'd always been more than willing to help her with whatever problem she had—not that she expected anything in return, of course.

"I'm going to start asking around the council to see who saw what and when. I didn't get there until the room was already full. Can't imagine it would be easy to hide spiking an entire punchbowl—"

"You'd be surprised," Greeley said. "Some of the poisons out there need a thimbleful. And honestly, those are the ones you worry about because, if enough is ingested, you'd be in rougher shape than losing your lunch."

Lillie's brow furrowed. "Do you think we're dealing with someone who knows poisons? I mean, it wouldn't be Zena or anything, would it?"

"I don't think so, not when she caters to a lot of the fisherfolk up north," Fawn said. "Business isn't great for her right now, but it's not bad enough for her to start making people sick intentionally." She paused, letting out an uncharacteristically catty snort. "Not that she has the *skill* for that anyway."

"Right, well, that's something," Lillie said, trying not to zero in on who *could* be educated enough in things like poison—and the only new person in town. "I'm going to check in on the fisherfolk and ask some questions. Do you think I could take a few tinctures with me to grease the wheels?"

"Actually, that would be very helpful," Greeley said. "The Jacobs have another three they've yet to pick up, and I made another for the Kovens upstairs. I was going to have Wineke deliver them, but she's out campaigning."

"How's that going?" Lillie asked.

Greeley and Fawn glanced at each other. "I support whatever she wants to do," Greeley said. "But she's got a lot of work ahead of her—and not a lot of time to do it in. The folks from Lower

Silverkeep are sure to vote for her, of course, but those who returned from elsewhere? They don't really know her, and they may be more inclined to vote for someone else."

"We're going to be optimistic, though," Fawn said with a firm nod. "She's so personable. I'm sure she could win anyone over."

"Agreed," Lillie said, gathering the tinctures and checking their labels. "I'll be back in a bit. I hope you two can figure out what's in that punch."

Greeley inspected the liquid again then gave Lillie a sideways look. "There's also a good chance the poison wasn't in the punch, you know."

"Believe me, that thought has crossed my mind, too," Lillie said. "But we don't have any pastries left, so this is our best first step."

~

Lillie's first stop was the Kovens upstairs. She'd been by briefly earlier that day to make sure everyone was doing all right but hadn't stopped to chat much.

Ursil answered, his cheeks still on the green side. "Ah, Lillie," he said, leaning on the door. "What can I do for you?"

"Just came by to bring your anti-nausea tincture from Greeley," Lillie said, gesturing to the basket. "And a bit of bread, if you think you can stomach that?"

Ursil opened the door wider, and Lillie followed him into his small front room. The Kovens' apartment was a mirror image of hers, with everything on the opposite side. Nikola was under the covers, her dark skin pale and wan.

"How are you?" Lillie asked, handing her the other vial.

"Rough," Nikola said, popping the cork and drinking. "I can't get out of bed. I doubt anyone can who was there last night."

"Except Jarvis, of course," Ursil said darkly. "Wouldn't put it past him to poison us."

"You think it's poison?" Nikola said with a frown to Ursil.

"Greeley has a bit of the punch from last night to test for all manner of things," Lillie said. "Hopefully, he'll be able to figure out exactly what's made everyone so ill." She hesitated. "Have there been, erm, any other symptoms, Nikola?"

She jumped as if Lillie had struck her. Nikola was part nymph, which gave her a leg up in the fishing industry because it allowed her to find fish with preternatural precision. If Jan McTavish was leaving pink fairy dust all over the place, there was a good chance Nikola was also suffering from a little enhanced magic.

"Relax, dear," Ursil said softly. "Lillie already knows, remember?"

"Oh, right," Nikola said, exhaling. "Then yes, as a matter of fact. My magic's been acting strangely."

Lillie nodded at her to continue.

"I'm not near the water," Nikola began, "but I can tell you exactly where every school of fish around Silverkeep Wharf is." She swallowed. "I usually need to be on the water itself to sense it. I thought maybe I was imagining things, but..."

"Are you having any trouble?" Ursil asked.

Lillie shook her head. "I think the person who did this was after more than disrupting the council. I think they were trying to expose magical secrets."

"That would make sense," Ursil said. "The McTavishes would be hard-pressed to let Nik keep her slip if everyone found out she could sense where the fish were. Jarvis would be leadin' the charge to get her expelled from the wharf."

"Ursil and I got there after you, Nikola," Lillie said. "Who was already there?"

"Most everyone, I'm afraid," she said. "Jarod Dupont and I got into a chat. He was hoping, since I was in with the McTavishes, I could help put a good word in for him about moving his booth. But other than that, I didn't speak with anyone else."

"Can you remember if you saw anyone around the punchbowl?" Lillie asked.

"Only the Jacob twins," Nikola said with a small laugh. "But I think they were hankering for something to eat, to be honest. They're always in your shop, aren't they?"

Lillie nodded. "Still, maybe they've got a secret vendetta against magical people."

"And still buy from a magical bakery every day?" Ursil asked.

"I'm not saying it makes total sense, but it's worth asking about anyway," Lillie said with a small laugh. "What about Kathryn Harkness? Did you see her near the food at all?"

"No, but I can't say I was looking out for her," Nikola said. "She's dreadful, isn't she?"

Appreciation warmed Lillie's chest. "Indeed. Can I bring you two anything else? I've got another couple loaves of bread down in the bakery, and a few more rising."

"This bread's pretty much the best thing I've ever eaten," Ursil said. "But maybe that's the tincture talking. I wouldn't say no to a few more slices."

"Feel free to help yourselves," Lillie said. "I think I'm going to be out and about the rest of the day. No use in staying open when half my customers are home sick, you know?" That, and she had a vested interest in finding out who'd done this—and make sure they didn't do it again. "I'm glad the tinctures are working. Your colors have improved dramatically."

"I don't feel completely well, but I'm much better—though I can still sense the fish," Nikola said. "I wonder how long the effects of that part of the potion will last."

"Hopefully, Greeley will find us an answer to all our questions," Lillie said. "You two get some rest and let me know if you think of anything else."

The Jacob twins lived across the street, above Jeremias Scarp's merchant office, in a setup that resembled Lillie's and the Kovens'. Glen, the single twin, lived in the smaller side apartment and Paul and his wife Evangeline lived on the larger side. Lillie didn't think any of the three had any kind of magic, though the twins were close enough that Evangeline often joked she was married to both of them. Lillie was on good terms with her, though a batch of anti-nausea tinctures would certainly be more welcome than the pobyd's usual pastry delivery.

Lillie rapped on the door, and Evangeline answered, looking exhausted. "Oh, goodness, what a surprise. Come in!"

"I come bearing gifts from Greeley Sloos," Lillie said, tapping the basket. "And I wanted to check on you folks. How's everyone faring?"

"I don't know what was in that stuff last night, but it certainly did a number on the boys," Evangeline said, gesturing to the two lumps covered in blankets on matching couches. Glen was heavy-lidded with a bowl next to him, and Paul was curled in a ball on the other side, moaning slightly. Evangeline tutted and quickly administered the potion, which seemed to breathe life back into both men.

"Thank goodness for Greeley," Evangeline said, standing next to Lillie as she watched her two charges. "I swear, I've never seen either of them this sick before. Poor dears."

"Anything else other than being sick?" Lillie asked. "I've, erm, heard some rumors that people with a speck of magic in their blood have seen some interesting reactions."

Evangeline frowned and shook her head. "No. The boys don't have any magic as far as I'm aware. And nothing new, either. Just sick."

"Well, now that you mention it," Glen said, sitting up slightly.

"Don't mention it, Glen," Paul said.

They shared a secret conversation with looks, and Evangeline threw her hands up in frustration. "Well, there's that. That's somewhat new."

"What are they doing?" Lillie asked.

"We're arguing, obviously," Glen said, scowling at Lillie.

"Obviously," Evangeline said with a dismissive snort. "You're staring at each other."

Paul, whose color was improving, frowned. "No, we're…talking. Can't you hear us?"

Lillie and Evangeline shook their heads.

The twins stared at each other, confused, then Glen groaned and covered his head with the blanket. "Whatever."

"Back in Pigsend, there was an artist who had a connection with his brother kind of like this," Lillie said. "I've had a few, erm, conversations with some people—not naming names, of course—but they've had similar issues pop up this morning. Never had a lick of magic, but after ingesting the punch, suddenly they've got a spark of it."

"Must've been some punch," Evangeline said. "The twins have been close, of course. They've been able to *almost* read each other's minds. But never like this."

Lillie sat on one of the chairs opposite them. "If you two feel up to it, I wanted to ask what you saw last night, especially before I got there. I heard you two were nearest the food table. Did you see anything out of the ordinary?"

"Well, we were there pretty early, but Jarvis was there before anyone else," Glen said.

"And based on how smug he was lookin', I wouldn't put it past him to have tried to usurp the McTavishes," Paul said. "Didn't escape my notice that *he* wasn't pukin' his guts up last night."

"But why would he be so obvious about it?" Evangeline asked.

"Because he's not the sharpest knife in the drawer," Paul said with a chuckle. "Which is why he doesn't have a slip anymore."

"He used to have one?" Lillie asked.

"Oh, yeah," Glen said with an emphatic nod. "There was a big shuffle last year, and both Jarvis and Lawson Dritter lost their spots. They sell Hipolita's fish now, but I know they'd both like to get back on the water themselves. They blame the Kovens, though it really wasn't their fault. Nikola's better at fishing. Can't help it if they couldn't find fish in a barrel if they tried."

That certainly explained why Jarvis wanted the McTavishes off the council. "Has Jarvis spoken to you about his campaign at all?"

"Not really, but I think he knows he's wasting his breath," Paul said. "We like the McTavishes, though I do wish they'd push back more on Mr. Globe's fees for the dock. They just went up again this year, and it's getting a bit ridiculous. Especially because, well, we don't even know if Mr. Globe owns the whole dock, you know?"

The McTavishes had said something similar, too. "What do you mean?" Lillie asked, feigning ignorance.

"Before the queen's folks came through," Glen said, "the dock was owned by the Town of Silverkeep, and whatever fees and whatnot were paid to keep the dock running, not to line anyone's pockets. Then the queen came to power, cleared out the town completely, and there weren't any boats coming at all. Mr. Globe said he purchased the wharf outright, and then did a bunch of repairs, and suddenly, the wharf was full of ships again."

"His ships," Paul said pointedly. "And anyone who wanted to use *his* wharf would have to pony up."

"The McTavishes were the only fisherfolk at the time, but as soon as Mr. Abora started inviting more of us, it got unwieldy, and the McTavishes created the council to work directly with Mr. Globe," Glen said. "Any of us who lived in Mr. Globe's properties got a discount on our dock fees."

"Until you moved out," Lillie said.

"Then we got hit with new dock fees," Glen said

darkly. "Which went up again. We went to the McTavishes to complain, and they said they were working on it. I suppose that's part of why they had a falling-out with Mr. Globe, and he hired a campaign manager for Jarvis."

Lillie tapped her finger to her chin. "If they couldn't fix it, would you vote for Jarvis?"

The twins shared a look and another silent conversation—if their wagging eyebrows were any indication.

"I...think I might," Glen said.

"If we had assurances we'd get a break on the dock fees, of course," Paul added quickly. "Jarvis talks a lot, but whether he could actually do anythin'... I mean, he might've been talkin' badly about Mr. Globe last night, but if Mr. Globe is payin' for that campaign manager, I don't trust him as far as I can throw him."

"Is that a common sentiment amongst the fisherfolk, you think?" Lillie asked.

"Nobody likes Mr. Globe," Evangeline said. "But he's been a necessary evil. I think most of the fisherfolk want to stay out of politics, keep their heads down, and pay as little as possible to whomever they need to."

"If I were you, I'd be findin' Jarvis Collin and askin' *him* what he knows," Glen said with a scowl.

"Where does he live, anyway?" Lillie asked. "He

wasn't at the wharf today. Ursil said he works for Hipolita, and she didn't seem in any state to fish today, either."

"He lives beneath Hipolita," Evangeline said. "Either she sublets to him, or he's got his own deal with Mr. Globe."

"Thank you," Lillie said after Evangeline gave her the details of how to find her home. "Greeley said he's making a few more tinctures, if you're in need. I'll head up to talk with Jarvis and see if I can't make any headway with him." She rose and surveyed the two patients. "I hope this passes quickly. I know the McTavishes are hoping to finish the discussions at tomorrow's meeting with the mayors."

"I hope they aren't planning on providin' any food or drink this time," Glen said with a groan. "I don't think I can stomach anythin' more than crackers."

"No offense, Ms. Dean," Paul said.

Lillie forced a smile, trying *very* hard not to zero in on the idea that someone was out to sabotage *her*.

~

There was more life in the Silverkeep town square, centered mostly around Globe Café. Lillie forced herself to look anywhere but there, trying to rid her mind of its handsome proprietor, but it was no use. She'd been too distracted last night and this morning to pen her response to Julian, and she wasn't quite sure what she'd say if she did.

*Hey, Julian. Miss you. What's the deal with your ex-girlfriend being a campaign manager? Oh, and are you kissing her? I hear you're good at that.*

She shook her head, amused at her own silliness. Julian was a grown man, and Lillie was a grown woman. She hadn't exactly *dated*, but she'd certainly kissed a few people in her time. It was ridiculous to be jealous, and yet... Yet it didn't fail to settle uncomfortably in her stomach that Julian would be free to date Kathryn if he so chose, whereas Lillie—

"Here to poison me?"

Lillie's thoughts were dashed abruptly when she realized she'd already walked all the way to Jarvis's house and knocked on his door. She blinked at him, a small blush rising to her face, until she registered what he'd said.

"Excuse me, I poisoned *no one*," Lillie stammered before she could stop herself.

"You know how it is," he continued, leaning onto the doorframe. "Long day at the bakery. You maybe put a few rotten eggs in the mix—"

"I would *never*," Lillie said with a gasp.

"I doubt anyone at the wharf will ever go to your place again after that," Jarvis said.

"That's an interesting thing to say," Lillie said with a tight smile. "One might think it's an admission of guilt."

He blanched. "W-what do you mean? I didn't do anything. I mean… I wouldn't—"

Lillie leaned in closer. "You would if it was on the orders of Mr. Globe."

"I don't take orders from him," Jarvis snarled.

"But you're using his campaign manager," Lillie said.

Jarvis looked honestly confused. "I don't know where she came from. But she showed up at my booth one day and started telling me what I was gonna do. I wasn't even gonna run for council, not when everyone *loves* the McTavishes, but she insisted and told me I was a shoo-in to win."

"Did she now?" Lillie crossed her arms over her chest. "Why'd she say that?"

"Because she said the McTavishes lost favor with Mr. Globe, I guess. She said if I did exactly as she said, she'd guarantee I got my dock slip back and make sure that every single fisherfolk voted for me."

Lillie already had a low opinion of Ms. Kathryn Harkness, but now it was getting downright abysmal. "I heard from the Jacob twins that you were the first one at the Sad Hill Pub last night."

"Yeah, that don't mean nothin'. I was there with Ms. Harkness running through what I was gonna say to people. I didn't go anywhere near your pastries."

"What about the punch?" Lillie asked. "Because I'm pretty sure *that's* what was spiked."

"Didn't touch *neither*," he said, emphatically. "You should go talk to Clifton if you're so worried. He probably did it."

"I already did. Besides that, why would he want to poison the people who make up the lion's share of his business?" Lillie asked.

"Because he's, um… Because…"

Jarvis continued to sputter, and Lillie started to feel bad for him. *He's not the sharpest tool in the shed*, Glen had said. Lillie was starting to agree. Criminal mastermind, he was not.

"If I were you," Lillie said, "I would decline Ms. Harkness's involvement in your campaign. It's clear she's fighting dirty, and I don't think making everyone in the market sick is going to endear them to your campaign. Especially since you didn't succumb. Looks fishy."

"Well, can't help it that I'm the only one with common sense enough not to eat your magic-laced stuff," Jarvis said with a sniff. "But I ain't got to explain myself to you." He slammed the door in Lillie's face.

"What's all the racket?" Hipolita called from a window above. She spotted Lillie and frowned. "Oh, what are you doing here?"

Lillie clicked her tongue, digging in her pockets

and finding one remaining anti-nausea vial. "Brought this tincture from Greeley Sloos. Interested?"

She made a noise. "Come on up."

~

Lillie found the townhome quite charming and welcoming, and Hipolita didn't look quite as green as everyone else but gratefully took the tonic and downed it immediately.

"I'm happy to oblige," Lillie said, perching on the edge of the chair in a smartly decorated living room. "I'm glad to see you're up and about. The rest of the wharf isn't faring so well, you know. Except Jarvis, of course."

"Yes, well." She shifted. "I'm not much for sweets, and I only had a few sips of the punch. I'm sure the Jacob twins are suffering mightily. They had about four servings of cookies."

Lillie inched forward, hope surging in her chest. "So you didn't eat any of the cookies?"

"I ate half of one." She tilted her head. "Do you think it was the cookies or the punch?"

"I'm not sure. There aren't any pastries left, but Greeley Sloos is testing a cup that Clifton had from last night," Lillie said. "The McTavishes asked me to get to the bottom of what happened."

"I'm sure they want that figured out," Hipolita said with a laugh. "They're already on the back foot as it is with all these dock fee increases."

"Were the fees before or after they decided to go against Mr. Globe?" Lillie asked conversationally.

Hipolita snorted as she settled into her seat. "After, of course. A few of us told 'em it was a bad idea to kick the hornet's nest, but the McTavishes felt that Mr. Globe wasn't nearly as powerful as he used to be. Now we've got a council election that's an actual race, with Jarvis swearing up and down he can do what the McTavishes can't."

"Do you believe him?"

Hipolita shrugged. "I think he'll be an admirable stooge for Mr. Globe, and if you ask me, Mr. Globe would like to keep his control of the fisherfolk. So if Jarvis wins, things would probably go back to the way they were a few weeks ago. Same slips, same dock fees. Not the best situation for us, but not the worst one, either."

"And if the McTavishes win?"

"It all hinges on whether he actually owns the wharf or not," Hipolita said. "I think if the McTavishes win, we're stuck with higher fees and the same number of slips in the interim, though. Certainly gives one something to think about."

Lillie chewed on this a moment.

"To answer the question I'm sure you came here to ask," Hipolita said with a smirk. "I don't think Jarvis poisoned everyone last night. He's an idiot, but he's not out to hurt anyone."

"Even if that poison resulted in some folks' secrets being revealed?" Lillie asked. "Magical ones?"

Hipolita considered that for a moment. "Well, that is interesting. We all have our theories about Nikola Koven, of course. No one brings in that much fish without having a leg up, you know?"

"What about other secrets?" Lillie asked. "Magic people might not have told anyone about."

"Bah. Those kinds of secrets don't have the weight they used to. The whole south side of Silverkeep is crawling with magical people. You're a pobyd, ain't ya?"

"I am, but—"

"If Nikola Koven stood up at the next Fisherfolk Council and announced she was part mermaid, I don't think anyone would bat an eye. And if anyone else stood up and announced they were part… I don't know, winged bat, I don't think they'd be too upset, either. The folks down at the wharf are concerned with getting dock slips and paying less gold to Mr. Globe. Magical abilities aren't really that important to us anymore."

Lillie nodded. "Well, even if that wasn't their intent, whoever poisoned the crowd surely meant to disrupt things. Thank you for your time." She reached into her pocket but found it empty. "Drat. I thought I'd leave you with another tincture. Greeley

Sloos has made a gigantic batch of them, if you're still feeling poorly."

"If Zena Plotter saw me down there, she'd have my head," Hipolita said with a laugh. "I'm okay here. Thank you, Lillie."

Lillie left the row of townhouses north of town, letting the sun warm her face as she headed back to the bakery. There was a lot swimming in her mind, of course, and a good walk was usually the thing to break some things loose. She wasn't ready to pin the blame on Kathryn, even though she really, *really* disliked her. But Lillie's personal dislike wasn't evidence of a crime, as much as Lillie wished otherwise.

She spotted the Silverkeep Inn, which had been completely restored to its former glory thanks to Reginald. Presumably, Kathryn would be staying there, which meant Noemi Lyle, the innkeeper, might be able to impart some information about her plans or things she might've said in passing.

Noemi was at the front desk and smiled warmly when Lillie walked inside. "Hey, Lillie. What brings you up this way?"

"I needed to borrow some paper for a letter," Lillie said, hoping that sounded realistic and not an excuse she pulled from thin air. "I'm all out and need to write some friends in Pigsend."

Noemi gave her a sideways glance but produced the asked-for items anyway. "How are things? Haven't seen you up this way since the mushroom debacle."

"I don't suppose you heard about the Fisherfolk Council last night, did you?"

When Noemi shook her head, Lillie told her everything she knew so far, including her suspicions that someone had poisoned the punch at the Sad Hill Pub—without mentioning she suspected Kathryn.

Noemi gasped and covered her mouth, so clearly this information hadn't reached this part of town yet. "Goodness. *All* the fisherfolk got sick?"

"Everyone except Jarvis," Lillie said. "And Kathryn."

Noemi blanched. "Why was she down there?"

"Apparently, helping Jarvis with his campaign to

unseat the McTavishes. Another Mr. Globe special," Lillie drawled, hoping this was the segue to get Noemi to spill the beans about Kathryn.

"That's strange. I thought he liked the McTavishes," Noemi said with a thoughtful tap to her chin. "And even stranger that he'd be so blatant about interfering with the Fisherfolk Council. He normally lets them do their thing, as long as he gets his gold."

"So I gather," Lillie said. "I also hear the McTavishes are trying to wrest some of that control back, which is why Mr. Globe's put his faith in Jarvis."

"And probably why he's got that campaign manager working for both him and Clancy," Noemi said with a shake of her head.

"What can you tell me about this campaign manager?" She shifted, hoping she sounded nonchalant and not at all like she was fishing for information about Julian's ex-girlfriend.

"She's...interesting," Noemi said after a moment's thought. "Definitely a big city sort of woman with big city expectations. I think it's only because Julian's next door that she isn't demanding I bring her breakfast in bed every day."

Lillie tapped the counter. "She's spending a lot of time with Julian, then?"

"I mean, that's where she's been coaching

Clancy," Noemi said, eyeing her with a half-smirk. "Why?"

"No reason."

"Does this have anything to do with the fact that she and Julian used to date in Sheepsburg?"

It took every bit of self-control not to grimace. "No, it absolutely does not."

"Then why have you turned into a tomato?" Noemi asked, her smile widening.

"Jan and Orxan McTavish asked me to look into what happened last night," Lillie said with some force. "She doesn't seem like she's willing to play fair."

"No, she doesn't," Noemi said. "She's already convinced half the town that Mr. Abora's the reason for all their problems—even if he had nothing to do with them. Kemp's been trying to shore up his support, but..."

"Do you know what happened between him and Mr. Globe?" Lillie asked. "Was it Mr. Globe's decision, or Mr. Abora's?"

"I don't know the details of that, to be honest," Noemi said. "Mr. Globe hasn't had a lot of faith in Kemp for weeks now, but if you ask me, Mr. Abora was the one to end their business relationship. I think he's ready to run the town the way he wants to, not what suits Mr. Globe the best."

"I can see why Mr. Globe wouldn't like that,"

Lillie said. "But why Clancy? He does a steady business in his butcher shop, doesn't he?"

"I hear he's looking to ease into retirement," Noemi said. "He sold his farm, and he and his wife moved into the apartment above his butcher shop, since it was vacant after the Jacobs moved out. Mr. Globe's convinced him to stick around and remain the town butcher until a replacement can be found, but I know he's angling for a much cushier job." She chuckled. "His wife is fuming though."

"Why?"

"Well, it was her family's farm they sold," Noemi said. "They didn't have any children or family nearby, so they had to sell to strangers. It sounds to me like Prunella is having second thoughts, especially after the new owners made a bunch of changes to their farm."

Lillie nodded. If Clancy's wife was having doubts about him running for mayor, maybe she was the next person to speak with. "Thanks for the information, Noemi. If you hear anything else, will you let me or Rey know? There's bound to be someone talking about it at dinner tonight." She turned and marched toward the door.

"Ah, Lillie?"

"What?" Lillie spun around.

Noemi picked up the letter and envelope Lillie had come in here to ask her for. "Don't forget these."

"Right." She flushed as she walked up to the counter. "Because that's the whole reason I came here." She cleared her throat as she took the items. "Thanks very much."

~

Although Clancy Cast was the only butcher in Silverkeep, Lillie hadn't had much opportunity to visit his shop. She didn't eat much meat in general, and when she did, it was because Nikola and Ursil had invited her to a delicious fish dinner. She approached the butchery with trepidation, pushing open the door and finding a delightfully rosy-cheeked woman with curly gray hair standing at the booth—Clancy's wife, Prunella.

"Good morning—ah. Lillie Dean." The cheery demeanor disappeared immediately. "What can I do for you?"

"Good morning, Prunella," Lillie said. "I was hoping to find Ms. Harkness. Is she around?"

"No." She crossed her arms over her chest. "They're over at Globe Café. Rehearsing. Again. Leaving me to handle the business here."

"I'm sorry to hear that," Lillie said. "Noemi tells me you've given up your farm?"

She made a dismissive sound. "Ridiculous. Clancy tells me that this smooth-talking consultant will ensure he wins the mayoral election, and then we won't have to work. I told him I'd rather not give up our entire business before all the votes are counted. Sure, we can count on the folks who live on this side of town to vote for him, but what about everyone else?"

"Wait, you sold your farm *after* he decided to run for mayor?"

"That Harkness woman swore it was the right call. I wouldn't be surprised if she was working for the person we sold it to, for all that she razzle-dazzled us." She waved her hands in the air as she mimicked Kathryn's quick and nasal tone. "Oh, it's the best idea. Nobody wants to vote for someone with their loyalties split. You'll want to move to town proper so you can be amongst your people." She scoffed. "And meanwhile, it's my family farm that's now in the hands of some…some stranger." She sighed. "We'd considered selling to the Honeygolds, but they can't even afford their own farm at the moment. Last I heard, Charla was thinking of selling, too."

"They are?" Lillie frowned. She hadn't heard that from Kristin, but the dairy farmer had mentioned they had money troubles.

"Oh, yes. Especially with poor Kristin breaking her leg." Prunella tutted. "I hate to say it was divine timing, but it certainly seems that way."

"So who owns your farm now?" Lillie asked.

"I'm honestly not sure," she said. "Some very well-dressed gentleman with a lot of jargon who paid us a nice sum of gold. One of Kathryn's friends, probably. They're cut from the same cloth."

"I bet it's hard to see your family's farm in someone else's hands," Lillie said.

Prunella scoffed. "I won't lie, the gold was nice. I was sure they'd overpaid, but they said our farmland was perfect for whatever it was they needed." She gestured around them. "We're still getting a supply of meat from a farm way outside of town, but it's not the same." The butcher let out a forlorn sigh. "I miss waking up in my own bed. This place is fine, but it's not home. I'm sure as soon as Clancy becomes mayor, this'll turn into something else. Noemi will convert to making fish dinners at the inn, and we'll live above what used to be my family's legacy."

"I'm so sorry," Lillie said, and meant it. It was clear Prunella hadn't been completely on board with the decision to uproot her life.

"Goodness, *I'm* sorry," Prunella said, shaking her head. "Prattling on like this. Did you need something? A cut of meat, perhaps? We've got some nice beef that might be good in a flaky, buttery crust. Came in from nearly two hours away, but—"

"That's all right," Lillie said, thinking quickly until she landed on a reason to be there that wasn't the truth. "I was… I'd also heard the Honeygolds were thinking of selling their farm and wanted to see about your rates for milk and eggs. But since you've sold your farm, suppose that's a moot point, isn't it?"

"Unfortunately," she said. "But even if we still had the farm, Mr. Globe has…erm… Well, he was quite clear about… Ah…"

Lillie frowned. "About what?"

"He'd asked us not to sell to you," she said. "Just after you moved to town. He made us sign an exclusive agreement to only sell to Globe Café."

"I see." Lillie tried not to take that personally. "Well, it doesn't matter anyway. I'll have to hope the Honeygolds don't sell their farm, or I'll be in trouble."

She nodded. "Indeed. Have a good day, Ms. Dean."

~

With no small amount of trepidation, Lillie headed back toward the bakery, chewing on all she'd learned and unable to shake the very loud part of her that insisted Mr. Globe was doing all he could to run Lillie out. She'd been so insistent that the punch had made everyone sick, but what if someone *had* sprinkled the poison on her pastries instead (or both, for that matter)? She'd certainly seen a drop in her business today, and even the McTavishes had said it would be a few days before they'd be comfortable eating her pastries again.

Much like Wineke needed the magicals and the fisherfolk to win the mayoral election, Lillie needed the fisherfolk to patronize her business to keep it running. If she lost half her revenue, she'd be forced to close shop and head back to Pigsend—perhaps exactly what Mr. Globe wanted. She envisioned him installing another baker in Lillie's deserted shop and balled her fists in indignation until she remembered he had no jurisdiction, because Rey was the true owner of her building.

But that didn't mean she wouldn't have to leave if she couldn't afford to buy flour or sugar.

Her attention drifted to Globe Café, and a new thought entered her mind. She and Julian were already bartering with chocolate and cinnamon. If Lillie lost the Honeygolds, perhaps they could swap milk and eggs instead. It would mean a little less money for Lillie, but she might actually get to see Julian more…

The thought made her smile.

"Ms. Dean!"

Mr. Abora jolted Lillie out of her thoughts, and she spun around to find him jogging over to her. "Mr. Abora, good afternoon."

"Good afternoon," he said, a little breathlessly. "I'm glad to see you. I was afraid you'd forgotten."

Lillie blinked at him, clearly having done that. "Erm, what?"

"Our… I mean, I have that event tonight, remember?" Mr. Abora said with a nervous smile. "Two dozen buttercream cupcakes. All bought and paid for. Remember?"

Lillie's eyes widened. "Oh, my goodness. Yes. Of course. Let me head back to the bakery. I'll have them to you within…two hours. At most. Will that work?"

A relieved smile broke across his face. "Thank you. I'm so grateful. Everything else seems to be going poorly for me. I'm worried Mr. Globe has made it his personal mission to ensure my campaign fails miserably."

"I understand the sentiment completely," Lillie said darkly. "Don't worry. I'll have everything ready to go well in advance of your meeting tonight. They'll be absolutely delectable."

And she'd have to make sure she kept an eye on them—just in case someone *was* out to get *her* and not put his thumb on the fisherfolk election.

"Right. Two dozen cupcakes."

Lillie started with her dry ingredients—flour, leavening, salt—while the milk was turning to butter in a bowl. She was grateful she'd grabbed a few jugs from Esmerelda earlier in the day, because that meant she didn't have to make another unpleasant walk to the wharf.

Then again, last time Lillie had been there, even Esmerelda had called it a day, so Lillie would've really been in trouble.

She combined the butter with sugar until it was nice and fluffy then added eggs one at a time, whipping the mixture thoroughly before incorporating the vanilla bean paste. As soon as the mixture was combined, she dabbed her pinky into the silky batter and tasted it, closing her eyes and sensing.

No, nothing piquing her pobyd senses. Not that she'd thought that would be the case.

"Thank goodness." She sighed, grabbing her scoop to evenly distribute the batter into the tins. She was still hopeful the punch would provide the answer, but in case… Well, she couldn't imagine making another campaign rally audience sick.

The familiarity of mixing and measuring and leveling calmed some of the lingering tension in Lillie's mind, and by the time she opened the oven to push the two tins inside, she was practically beaming. She'd turned to start on the buttercream when a shadow emerged from the mousehole on the ground, his noise pointed at the sky.

"Oh, goodness, are we baking? Bit late in the day for that, isn't it? And you've got an entire case filled with stuff, don't you?"

"Mr. Abora's cupcakes for his election event tonight," Lillie said, opening the oven and sticking the cupcake tins inside. "I forgot completely, what with all the fisherfolk council stuff I've been investigating today."

"Have you had any luck?" Rey asked.

"Don't have a culprit, but I'm putting together a picture of things," Lillie said. "What about you?"

"About the same," Rey said, settling himself on the edge of the counter as Lillie took another jug and made buttermilk with it. "That Kathryn Harkness is certainly making a name for herself. She and Clancy have been practicing nonstop at the Globe Café for the past few days. And when she's not with him, she's haranguing Jarvis about his talking points, which are usually similar." Rey shook his head.

"Okay, I know all that," Lillie said. "What about the Fisherfolk Council meeting last night? Surely, there's been some conversation about that."

"Everyone knows about it, of course, but no one had anything new to share because nobody's living or dining at the Sad Hill Pub," Rey said. "There are, of course, seagulls and terns and the like who nest nearby, but nobody's actually *in* the pub to overhear anything. Not like the Silverkeep Inn, you know."

"Of course," Lillie said.

"The birds overhear conversations at the wharf, but all the fisherfolk were at home recovering today, so there was no conversation to be had," Rey continued. "The bartender isn't very welcoming to us small folk, you know. Last time I was there, I almost got caught in a run of the mill mouse trap. Could you imagine?" He tutted. "I'd be shamed.

Couldn't claim the name Reynard Moussison anymore."

"I'm sure you could get by," Lillie said with a grin. "But more on topic, we've both been all over this town and don't have a single thing to show for it. The next Fisherfolk Council meeting is tomorrow, and the McTavishes asked me to find them an answer."

She plopped the butter into the bowl and added sugar, then beat them together with some milk, a little more vanilla bean paste, and a few large scoops of her cocoa powder. The buttercream combined beautifully, and Lillie's nose filled with the scent of delicious chocolate. She dipped her finger in and took a taste, smiling at the perfect flavor.

"Maybe something will pop open tomorrow, when all the fisherfolk are feeling better," Rey said.

"Tomorrow might be too late," Lillie said, glancing at the clock. "I was hoping Greeley would have an answer by now. I haven't been over to check yet—and I've got to get these cupcakes back up to Mr. Abora before his event starts. Goodness knows he needs all the help he can get."

"I thought you were voting for Wineke," Rey said.

"Of course I am," Lillie said. "But you know, he's such a..." She tried in vain for the right word. "He did invite me to Silverkeep. I have to give him credit for that, at least. And it's clear Mr. Globe is meddling in both the fisherfolk *and* the mayoral election—not to mention my own business."

She told him what she'd learned from Prunella about Kathryn telling them to sell the farm after Clancy had been recruited to run for mayor—as well as Mr. Globe banning them from selling anything to Lillie.

"That perfidious monster," Rey said. "He needs to be taught a lesson, Lillie, I mean it."

Lillie made a noncommittal noise. She didn't disagree, but she wasn't going to be the one to teach the merchant anything—least of all when she still owed him. "Hopefully, Greeley has an answer soon."

"Hm. You know, it's awfully convenient that Clifton had that cup," Rey said. "What if Clifton *knew* there was an apothecary in town, so he set aside a small amount of unpoisoned drink, knowing you'd be by to pick it up and test it!"

Lillie quirked a brow. "That's an awful lot of ifs, Rey. And Clifton's main business comes from the fisherfolk and sailors at the wharf. He wouldn't do anything to jeopardize that."

"Exactly why he'd want to cover his tracks," Rey said with a smirk. "See, Lillie, I should always be involved in these things because I notice things you don't, eh?"

"Or you come up with wildly outlandish

theories that don't have any basis in reality," Lillie said with a shake of her head. "Tell me what's going on at the Silverkeep Inn. No detail is too small."

Rey, of course, was a fount of knowledge as it related to gossip and rumor mills, but except for a long diatribe about Kathryn Harkness being persnickety, there was nothing new in his screed. Lillie listened as she cooled the cupcakes and iced them, making sure that she took extra time to pipe the decoration gorgeously. She was finishing the last bit when the door opened, and Greeley came in.

"Hey, Lillie," he said. "I hope I'm not interrupting."

"Not at all." She put down the icing bag and joined him in the front room, with Rey perched on her shoulder. "Did you discover anything?"

"Unfortunately, no," he said with a loud sigh. "We tested it for everything under the sun—including a few things Fawn thought of. And both of us had a taste of it, too." He gestured to himself. "No issues. I don't think the problem was in the punch."

"Or not in *that* punch," Rey said. "I declare, we should go back to that bartender, and—"

"Or the culprit sprinkled something onto the pastries while they were left unattended for a few hours," Lillie said, causing Rey to clam up. "Because someone wanted to disrupt the council and also possibly ruin my business at the same time."

"I could see that," Greeley said, nodding slowly. "I wish we had a sample we could test, but..."

"I get it." Lillie looked back at the cupcakes in the kitchen. "I've been testing and tasting these as I go, and I haven't had a single issue."

"More cupcakes?" Greeley frowned.

"For Mr. Abora's campaign rally. Don't mention it to Wineke, or she'll be mad at me again," Lillie said. "I suppose I've got to stay in the room and keep an eye on them, don't I? Can't let it happen again."

"I'll join you," Rey said. "Two pairs of eyes are better than one!"

"Thanks, Greeley, for looking into it anyway," Lillie said.

Greeley smiled, though there was pity in it. "I'm sorry I couldn't be more help. But the good news is that everyone seems to have recovered from it. So no lasting effects, whatever it was." He glanced at the cupcakes, sitting on the table behind her. "But I wouldn't leave anything edible alone until you figure out who's behind it."

~

With the clock ticking closer to the event start time, Lillie hastily boxed up the cupcakes, wrapping them in a little extra twine *in case*. Even though the cupcakes were covered, she was still jittery and jumpy—unable to get Greeley's warning out of her mind. Rey perched on her shoulder as she locked up the bakery (making sure the front *and* back doors were secure before leaving, of course), and she couldn't help but look around nervously, waiting for Kathryn to jump out of an alley and sprinkle poison on her cupcakes.

"Steady on, Lillie," Rey muttered. "We'll get these safely to Mr. Abora. No doubt about it."

With one hand pressed to the top of the box, and the other holding it in place, Lillie started up the hill. She gave passersby a wide berth—Edwina Featherswift gave her a sideways look—but thankfully, nobody stopped to talk with her.

"Lillie!"

She yelped in surprise, grateful she had a firm grip on the cupcakes, as she staggered backward. Tom, still human, jogged up behind her, a casual, friendly smile on his face.

"T-Tom. Goodness, you scared me," she said, keeping a wide space between them.

"Oh, I'm..." The brown-haired, pale man looked around then down at his hands. A trickle of guilt ran down Lillie's spine as he touched his face, perhaps searching for signs he'd been re-cursed.

"No, I meant," she said after a moment, "I was lost in thought and didn't hear you calling me. Sorry."

His smile relaxed. "I heard about what happened at the Fisherfolk Council. Greeley came over to ask if I knew of anything that causes a similar reaction."

Lillie shifted. "Do you?"

"There are lots of things that cause magical flares and sickness in regular folks," he said. "A whole host of flowers in the *pernellitina* family, you know. Unfortunately, that has a few hundred species in it, so it's not narrowing the list much." He rocked on his feet. "I don't suppose it really matters *what* did it as much as *who* did it, right?"

Lillie nodded. "I've got a few theories about that, too, but nothing concrete right now."

"I'm sure you do." Tom tilted his head at her. "Where are you headed, anyway? And with those cupcakes?" He leaned in closer. "They look scrumptious—"

Even though the pastries were well-covered, Lillie took a large step back. "For Mr. Abora's campaign rally this evening. With all the…well, I'm sure you can understand, I'm trying to make sure they arrive intact."

"Well, Lillie, you know I would *never*…" Tom frowned, genuinely hurt.

"It's not you, Tom. I'm just…" Lillie bit her lip. "This has to go well tonight. My business is already down significantly. And I just…" She swallowed. "It has to go well."

"I'm so sorry I haven't been by lately, but I'll be sure to stop in the morning. You've been nothing but kind to me, Lillie, and I'm happy to support." He nodded to the cupcakes. "And if I can be of service in finding out who's behind this awful poisoning, do let me know. I owe you."

"You don't. But I appreciate it." She glanced at the sky. "But I'm going to be on Mr. Abora's bad side if I don't get these cupcakes to the town hall in the next ten minutes, so..." She bobbed her head. "I'll see you around, Tom!"

She hated leaving him with a frown on his face—but it couldn't be helped. These cupcakes had to arrive at the town hall without a single problem.

Some of the tension left her shoulders as she approached the town square without any further interruptions. She spared the Globe Café a single glance but kept moving toward her main purpose. She was climbing the stairs when a tall shadow appeared next to her, and a pale hand landed on the door.

"Lillie Dean, what in the world are you doing on this side of town?" Benetta Pearlson was a magical seamstress who'd been down in Lower Pigsend with Lillie during the queen's reign. She was the only member of the returned group to reclaim her ancestral home, and thus the only magical who lived around the town square. She'd found her groove—especially since Odetta Globe had started buying dresses from her—and Lillie hadn't had much cause to chat with her lately.

"Mr. Abora asked me to bring some goodies to the event," Lillie said, plastering her hand atop the box. "What about you?"

"Ah, well, I felt bad for him. He's got no fans on this side of town." She shrugged. "And Roudie said I should come."

Lillie softened a hair. The local dock repairman carried quite a torch for Benetta, and while she was coy about the exact nature of their relationship, Mr. Roudie often stopped in after his workday to get *two* cookies from Lillie.

"Well, I know he appreciates it," Lillie said, holding the box close to her.

"I'm frankly surprised you're here. I didn't think you liked the man."

"I'm not saying I'm voting for him, but gold is gold." Lillie could be honest about that, at least. "Have you met Clancy's new campaign manager?"

Benetta made a disgusted face. "She's abysmal. Came into my shop no fewer than four times this week asking for outrageous pieces—then she showed up this afternoon and practically dragged me out of my shop to watch that butcher fumble through a whole speech over at Globe Café."

"You don't say?" Lillie said, resisting the urge to

ask if Julian had been there. "Was it interesting?"

"It's clear he's been coached. And I can smell a plant a mile away. He's there to do Mr. Globe's bidding. And as someone who's currently surrounded on all sides by Mr. Globe's properties, I'll tell you that I won't vote for *anyone* who has anything to do with him."

"Wineke Sloos is running, too," Lillie offered.

"She's nice and all," Benetta said with a sigh. "And I very much like that she's stuck it to Zena Plotter several times. But being on this side of town, I see a lot of what goes into Mr. Abora's job, and I don't think she understands what she's signing up for. Neither does Clancy, for that matter. Mr. Abora, at least, has some experience managing the town and its people. He did a terrible job when we all returned, but who could do a good one under the circumstances?"

Lillie bristled. *He could've written fewer blackmail letters.* "I suppose."

"And if he's fully out from Mr. Globe's thumb like he claims? Well, then I dare say he might even do better. But that would require him to grow a backbone, first. Jury's still out on that." She scoffed. "Which is why I'm giving him a chance to impress me tonight. If he can show he's got some courage stuck in that long hair of his, perhaps he might earn my vote."

*And if he doesn't, maybe Wineke has a shot after all.*

"Suppose we've been yapping out here long enough," Benetta said, finally opening the door. "Shall we?"

The town hall was far emptier than Lillie would've guessed, considering who was throwing the event. Mr. Abora was the most well-known of the three candidates, and while he'd had his share of issues, Lillie thought there'd be more folks who believed as Benetta did, that he was decent at a difficult job. Lillie chanced a look out into the audience. Benetta had found a spot next to Mr. Roudie, the dock repairman. Jeremias Scarp, Lillie's neighbor, sat in the same row, too. Reginald was there with Haruko, whose white tail was twitching behind her. Behind them were a few sailors from the merchant ships. But all in all, less than ten had come to hear Mr. Abora speak.

"Yikes," Rey muttered on Lillie's shoulder.

"Ah, Ms. Dean! You're right on time." Mr. Abora, wearing his nicest tunic and pants, scurried over to take the containers from her.

"If it's all the same to you, I'll get them set up," Lillie said, throwing a protective arm over them. "I..." She licked her lips. "I want to make sure the presentation is...perfect. You know how it is."

"Oh, of course, excuse me." Mr. Abora took a few steps back. "Well, I do expect the crowd to grow in the next few minutes, so be quick about putting them out."

Lillie chanced a look out in the audience. She certainly hadn't seen anyone on their way up the hill, but that didn't mean they weren't a few steps behind her.

"Right, well, I'll get to plating these."

Mr. Abora showed her to the table he'd set up for her, and Lillie put Rey down on it to keep watch as she carefully pulled each cupcake out and placed it on the table. "See anyone coming yet?"

"Not yet," Rey said. "Though they all look hungry. Maybe they should go ahead and snag a cupcake before anyone has a chance to do something to them."

"Right you are," Lillie said, stepping away from

the table. "Please, help yourselves. Courtesy of Mr. Abora."

The very small crowd rose from their seats and milled over, and Lillie kept a sharp eye on hands and coats. But no one as much as went for their pocket as they sidled up next to the table and chose their cupcake.

"I do love a chocolate cupcake," Benetta said, plucking one from the middle. "Perhaps a stroke of genius to invite you to bake instead of Julian."

Lillie gave her a thin smile but before she could respond, a harsh voice broke through the crowd. "Ah, I wouldn't touch those if I were you. I hear they're poisoned."

Lillie spun to find Kathryn Harkness standing ten paces away, grinning like the shark she was.

Rey let out a huff and marched toward the edge of the table. "Absolute slander! Lillie will see you in court for this!"

"I will not," Lillie said, giving him a meaningful glance. It wasn't as if she could afford a lawyer, let alone drag someone like Kathryn Harkness into a legal battle.

"Ms. Harkness, what a surprise to see you here," Mr. Abora said, looking neither surprised nor pleased that she'd made an appearance at his event. "We were about to get underway."

"Were you?" She gave Benetta a once-over, and

the seamstress returned it in spades. Lillie had never loved Benetta more. "Well, I figure someone has to warn the masses about your poisonous pobyd."

"Nobody has to..." Lillie licked her lips, keeping an eye on Kathryn's hands, in case she had a vial hidden there. "Don't tell me you're assisting Mr. Abora with his campaign, too?"

"Ah, hardly. I'm here to see if there's anything worth mentioning to Jarvis," she said with a loud and off-key laugh. "Or Clancy. I can't remember who's running for what. This town has too many people in it." She tossed a lock of her hair out of her face again—a signature move that was starting to grate on Lillie. "Anyway, Kell—"

"Kemp," Mr. Abora ground out.

"It doesn't matter," she said with that same dismissive chuckle. "I'd think twice about buying from that bakery. She's clearly not careful about her ingredients or her quality control. The entire Fisherfolk Council was sick from her cookies last night."

"That's...not true," Lillie forced herself to say.

"No, I heard that," Roudie piped up from the audience. "The whole wharf was struck down by some kinda mystery virus. Was it really your cookies, Lillie?"

Kathryn's grin widened as a blush rose up Lillie's cheeks. "Apparently someone decided to add something extra to them," Lillie said with some difficulty. "But I promise these cupcakes are perfectly fine to eat. I tested them repeatedly before I boxed them up." She leveled a glare at Kathryn. "And assuming no one else added anything…"

"I mean, who can trust a pobyd? Can you even get food poisoning from your own baked goods?" Kathryn laughed. "I hear it's not the first time you've added something to your goods. Isn't that right, Roudie?"

Mr. Roudie jumped as if not expecting to hear his (correct) name. "Erm. Well, I don't—"

"Hush, Roudie." Benetta elbowed him roughly.

"I'm just sayin'." Kathryn picked up a cupcake and sniffed it then made a face like it was rancid. "I wouldn't trust this pobyd as far as I could throw her." She chuckled and put the cupcake back down. "Consider that free advice. I'd normally charge three gold coins for that."

She laughed as she sauntered toward the door.

The gazes of everyone in the room were on Lillie, including those with chocolate around their mouths. She ran her tongue over her teeth and glared at everyone.

"I didn't poison *anyone*," she snapped. "But if you'll excuse me, I've got a bone to pick with *Ms. Harkness*."

~

Lillie all but ran out the door after the consultant, who was only a few steps down the town hall stairs. She didn't seem surprised when Lillie called her name and smiled as if she were protected by an impervious bubble of magic.

"Something you needed, Lils?"

Lillie almost tripped over her feet. That was Julian's nickname for her. She shook that off—as well as any questions about exactly what Julian had discussed with her—and squared her shoulders. "What's the big idea, telling everyone I poisoned the Fisherfolk Council?"

"You were there. Everyone was..." She made a disgusted face. "They ate your pastries not a few moments before."

"And the punch," Lillie said hotly. Of course, Greeley had confirmed there was nothing amiss there, but Lillie wasn't going to give Kathryn the satisfaction of knowing that.

"Yes, but I had a sip of that godawful punch," Kathyrn said, her eyes glittering with malice. "And look at me..." She gestured to herself. "Perfectly hale."

"Yeah, well, there was some left over," Lillie said, struggling to find a response to the consultant's self-satisfied expression. "I gave some to the local apothecary for him to test for toxins."

"And did he find anything?" She smirked like

she knew the answer.

"Well, no, but…" Lillie lifted her chin, deciding to use Rey's convoluted theory in the absence of anything else. "It's possible the glass I was given was poured before the poison was added."

"Wow, that's really a complicated theory, isn't it?" She laughed and kept walking toward Globe Café. "But I guess I shouldn't be surprised. I hear that's your thing."

Lillie gaped at her. "My *thing*?"

"Yeah, solving all these little magical mishaps," she continued, turning and observing Lillie as if she were a child. "Poking around where nobody wants you. Heroically uncovering the ne'er-do-wells who mean to bring harm to this quaint little town." Kathryn grinned at Lillie's stunned expression. "Kinda like with that amulet thing? And the solstice celebration? And, what was it recently…something about mushrooms?"

"How did you…?"

"It's my job to know everything about a town I'm working in," she said. "Besides that, Julian and I had a long chat about you."

Lillie couldn't help the breath that puffed out of her lips. "About me?"

"I mean, I've spoken to a *lot* of folks since I first got here. And *your* name came up again and again." She grinned like a cat surveying a baby bird. "You, missy, have a reputation."

"I'm a baker," Lillie said with as much force as she could muster. "If I *happen* to get involved in other things, it's because someone's asked me to help them and, for whatever reason, they don't feel comfortable going to Sheriff Juno." Lillie crossed her arms over her chest. "Or because someone's got a vendetta against me and my business."

"Do they?" She fluttered her eyelashes. "And who is this mysterious someone? Because it sounds like you just had a bad batch of butter."

"Butter doesn't cause the sort of sickness that happened to the fisherfolk yesterday," Lillie said. "It seems to me someone wanted to reveal secrets that could've cost the McTavishes their election."

Kathryn's brows wagged. "What kinda secrets? I confess I don't have much on them, other than the obvious. Would love to add to my arsenal."

Lillie couldn't believe she'd nearly revealed Jan's fairy secret. This woman truly had a knack for making Lillie crazy. "Not the McTavishes. Other people's secrets."

"Who?"

"Nobody."

"Then clearly, it wasn't the intention, if there are no secrets to reveal," Kathryn said with a noncommittal shrug. "This is fun, Lils, but—"

"Lil-*lie*," she snapped, anger clouding her mind.

"And I don't know what you told Julian about me, but—"

Kathryn smirked. "Would you like me to tell you? It was a very long, very *intimate* conversation. Early in the morning—bakers' hours, you know. Can't believe he threw away a perfectly good career and a lot of gold working for his father to play with pastry dough, but what do I know?"

Lillie was going to tear up that letter when she got home—though she couldn't exactly say why she was mad with Julian. "Whatever Julian may have told you—"

"As I said, he told me everything, and what he didn't tell me, I pieced together." She smirked. "Why do you think Audo brought *me* in, specifically?"

Lillie'd had her suspicions. "I'm sure I don't know."

"Oh, darling, I know you're a baker, but you can't possibly be that thick." She crossed her arms over her chest. "Or maybe you are. Who knows?" She chuckled. "I'm here for Julian, too. And believe me when I say I *always* get what I want."

The door opened before Lillie could respond, and Mr. Abora poked his head out. "Erm. If you two don't mind, I'm about to start my campaign rally, and everyone can hear your conversation. It's rather distracting."

"Sorry, Mr. Abora," Lillie said, though she didn't really feel it.

"Oh, I'm not. You're not going to say anything to them they don't already know about you," Kathryn said with a laugh. "If any of them want to come hear Clancy talk, we're having another rally at Globe Café in the morning." She winked at Lillie. "Sponsored by Julian, of course. And with non-poisoned pastries, too." She cackled as she headed down the street. "Good luck to you both. Hope you've got a trashcan nearby."

Mr. Abora stared at Lillie, and she balled her fists. "My pastries *aren't* poisoned."

"Of course not," he said, "but if you don't mind, since you're here... Could you listen in and round out my audience numbers?"

~

There really wasn't much rounding to be had. Lillie made eleven people total, including Rey, and the town hall was woefully underpopulated. Lillie sat in her own row, too agitated to sit next to Reginald or Benetta, or even Jeremias. As Mr. Abora launched into his stump speech about all the good things he'd done in Silverkeep, Lillie let her mind wander to everything Kathryn had said.

Even though she *knew* Kathryn was trying to rile her up, she couldn't help but *be* riled. She had very little impulse control where Julian was concerned, and something about Kathryn using Julian's pet name for her sent warning flags flying in her mind. Julian wasn't stupid, of course, and he did understand that his and Lillie's relationship (if they could even call it that) was forbidden.

But what if his affection for Lillie had gone out the door with the appearance of his old flame?

*"I always get what I want."*

Lillie very much wished she could sneak out, rap on the Globe Café's backdoor, and yell at him a little bit. But it was still early evening, and she'd be seen coming and going from his shop. Best to actually write that letter, and—

"Well, clearly," Mr. Abora said, "Lillie's endorsing me. Aren't you?"

Lillie's cheeks flushed as she came back into the room. "What was that?"

"He said you were endorsing him," Rey muttered, having climbed back onto Lillie's shoulder in her distraction. "What will Wineke think?"

Lillie could scarcely believe her ears but couldn't stop herself from standing up and padding toward the front of the room. Time seemed to move in slow motion, and yet before she had a coherent thought or argument, she was in front of the ten people (was it only ten? Now it looked like a thousand), all of them waiting to hear why Lillie endorsed Mr.

Abora.

"Well?" He smiled expectantly at her.

"Uh, well," Lillie began slowly. "I'm...impressed at how well you've handled the melding of the transplants and the returned. Including when Lower Silverkeep closed down."

"Right, that was me and Reginald," Mr. Abora said, gesturing to the mage. "So grateful to have your support."

Reginald, who looked the way Lillie was feeling, sank down into his chair. Haruko tutted at him.

"And...erm...if it wasn't for Mr. Abora, I wouldn't be here at all," Lillie continued, still trying for nice things to say that didn't necessarily constitute her endorsement. "I think he's done an admirable job as assistant mayor all this time."

"Which means you're voting for me, right?" Mr. Abora prompted. Then, when Lillie opened and closed her mouth, he leaned in to add, "You've got to say it, or they might think you're voting for someone else."

Lillie gave him a smile that she *hoped* conveyed her true feelings, but before she could say anything, Reginald coughed—and a large fireball erupted from his mouth.

"Oh, goodness!" Reginald cried, hopping to his feet as the fire took hold. But it hadn't come from him—Haruko's tail was burning white and setting the bench behind her on fire.

"What in the—?" Mr. Abora gaped before jumping into action. "We need water! Hand pumps —there's one at Globe Café and the Silverkeep Inn!"

"No need," Reginald said, whipping out his wand.

"No, wait!" Lillie barked, but it was too late. The small trickle of water Reginald had meant to conjure was more a gigantic splash, putting out the fire, but dousing everyone in the room.

Benetta shrieked, but not because her perfectly coiffed hair was dripping. Her skirts were whipping around her knees, threatening to expose her undergarments, and poor Mr. Roudie, dripping from Reginald's wave, was doing his best to keep her decent, with little success.

The sailors had bolted toward the door, but not before one of them had sprouted pointed ears.

And Lillie stood in the center of it all, water dripping from her body and nose, gaping at the chaotic scene, her mind buzzing with shock and horror.

"Well," Rey observed from Lillie's shoulder, "I suppose we can unequivocally say someone is out to sabotage *you*."

The chaotic scene died down quickly. Reginald, who'd figured out he probably shouldn't wield magic, was doing his best to steer clear of Haruko's white-hot tail. The kitsune was in tears, holding her tail and carefully inching toward the door, whimpering her apologies for setting everything on fire. Benetta and Roudie, still battling her misbehaving hemline, were next, arguing with each other about the best way to keep the skirts under control.

Then it was just Mr. Abora, Lillie, and Rey, who was still perched on her shoulder.

The assistant mayor turned toward her, his face growing dark with anger. "So Kathryn was right then? You're poisoning people?"

"I'm not. I mean—"

"Now see here," Rey said, marching as far forward on Lillie's shoulder as he could without toppling off. "Lillie is clearly being targeted. She didn't do a thing wrong—I watched her make these cupcakes. Someone clearly added something to them."

*Did they?* Lillie kept that thought—as well as her absolute certainty that no one had gotten between her and the cupcakes—to herself. "I'm so sorry, Mr. Abora. I wish I could tell you what happened. I took every precaution to make sure no one did anything to the cakes, but it's clear I wasn't…" She shook her head. She'd tasted them. She'd kept them safe. How in the *world* had someone poisoned them? "There's no excuse. I'm sorry. But please know this wasn't intentional. I wouldn't dream of disrupting your event like this."

"No?" He laughed hollowly. "Not even after I sent you blackmail letters?"

"Even so," Lillie said with a firm nod. "That's not how I operate."

"This is a disaster," Mr. Abora said, looking around the empty town hall, still dripping from Reginald's attempts to put out Haruko's fire. Three benches had gone up in flames, and several more had black marks on them.

"If it's the same thing that made the fisherfolk sick," Lillie said quietly, "then it'll wear off by tomorrow. Reginald will be able to put all this right, I'm sure—"

"Not the hall. My campaign. It's... Well, I suppose I should be thankful no one came." He rubbed his face. "But rumor will spread. Kathryn Harkness will make sure of that."

"Yes, she probably will," Lillie muttered.

Mr. Abora rubbed his face. "I'm going to have to... Well, I don't really have the money to..." He glared at Lillie. "You will, of course, be refunding me for the pastries."

"Of course," Lillie said quietly. There went more of her payment to Mr. Globe, but she couldn't, in good conscience, keep Mr. Abora's money after this.

"What am I going to do?" Mr. Abora whined to himself as he walked through the dripping wet town hall toward his office—then seemed to think better of it and walked out the door.

Lillie flinched as it shut behind him.

"Rey, this is bad," Lillie said, walking up to the table where her cupcakes sat. Thankfully, Reginald's water hadn't made it this far. "This is really, *really* bad. There wasn't a single person who could've put something in these cupcakes from the bakery to here, which means—"

"Someone's tampered with your bakery," Rey finished. "Is that even possible? You're so good at locking up behind you. And goodness knows, I'm always around."

"Not always," Lillie said with a knowing look. "And I honestly haven't a clue. But it's clear I can't bake anything else until Greeley discovers the source of it." She winced, thinking about all the gold she wasn't going to make. "Mr. Abora was right. This is a disaster."

"Look on the bright side," Rey said as she packed the cupcakes back into the box. "We know it's something in your pastries. You've got a plethora of samples to give Greeley for him to test. It was awful what happened in here, yes, but at least it gave us another clue."

Lillie picked up one of the offending cupcakes and scrutinized it closely. She'd tasted these multiple times as she'd worked and nothing had seemed out of the ordinary. She wasn't a stranger to magical spikes, having endured a few in Pigsend, but she had absolutely no doubt in her mind that these cupcakes were safe to eat.

But if that were the case, how could someone have poisoned them?

"Do you want me to walk back to the bakery with you?" Rey asked.

"No, you go to dinner," Lillie said, quickly boxing up the rest of the cupcakes. "Keep your ears open—especially where Kathryn is concerned."

Lillie lingered in the town square after they parted, replaying the events of the evening and reminding herself just how *careful* she'd been. Kathryn had appeared after everyone who'd gotten sick had taken a cupcake, so there was no way—unless she had some kind of invisibility magic—that she could've added anything without anyone seeing.

"Well, this is certainly an interesting wrinkle."

Benetta had changed out of her whirling skirts and into a pair of overalls that looked suspiciously similar to the ones Mr. Roudie had been wearing. The pant hems still flared as if they wanted to dance around, but thankfully, they stayed at her ankles.

"If you say one word about my outfit—" she began.

"Wouldn't dream of it," Lillie said quietly.

"It smells like fish, but at least I'm not in danger of flashing the entire town," Benetta said, squaring her shoulders. "Tell me the truth. Did you do this?"

"Absolutely not," Lillie said. "I truly have no idea what's going on. But—"

"But someone is out to ruin your business, dear, I hate to tell you," Benetta said. "Roudie told me all about the Fisherfolk Council. Good thing he wasn't there, or he'd have had a double dose of whatever this is. Man doesn't have a drop of magic in his bones, but he might now."

Lillie looked down at the cupcakes, still tightly boxed up. "I cannot fathom how they did it. These things never left my or Rey's sight."

"Well, you do have your share of enemies. Have you been to see Zena Plotter lately? She never has anything nice to say about you."

Zena *would've* been an apt suspect, except she was a terrible apothecary, and she still hadn't found an apprentice to make up for what she lacked. "I fear it might be bigger than her."

"Like who? Mr. Globe?" She quirked a brow. "He *hates* you for some reason."

"Have you spoken to him about me?" Lillie asked. Someone had told the merchant about Lillie's past in Lower Pigsend, and as Benetta had been there… "Did you tell him what I did in Lower Pigsend?"

Benetta gasped, covering her chest with her hand. "What do you take me for, Lillie? I may be making skirts for his daughter, but I'm not about to ally myself with that awful man. And I certainly wouldn't want to tell him *anything* about you." She lifted her chin. "I haven't told a single soul about it, thank you very much."

Some of the tension left Lillie's chest. "You don't know how much I appreciate that, Benetta."

"I take it he knows?" She snorted when Lillie nodded. "Well, maybe he asked one of the other people who lived there."

"I suppose it was only a matter of time." Her gaze drifted to Globe Café, a pang of sadness echoing in her chest. What she wouldn't give to go talk to Julian about all this and hear what he had to say. She *missed* him something awful.

*"I always get what I want."*

Would he even want to see her with Kathryn Harkness tempting him?

"Love troubles with Mr. Globe the younger?" Benetta asked to Lillie's silence.

Lillie's head snapped around. "N-no! I mean, that is to say... There's nothing going on—"

Benetta laughed with a knowing look. "Right, and Mr. Roudie brings me fresh-cut flowers every afternoon because he likes the way they look in my front room. And is currently wrapped in one of my robes because, as he said, 'Nobody cares about seeing my drawers.'" She tilted her head. "The *entire* town saw Julian carry you out of the Silverkeep Inn a few weeks ago."

"Not the entire town," Lillie muttered.

"Enough of the town. And those who didn't see it heard about it, I'm sure," Benetta continued, scrutinizing her reaction. "But...perhaps you don't feel the same about him?"

"No, I do—" Lillie closed her mouth before she dug herself deeper. "It's not about that."

"It's his father, then?" Benetta surmised with a sniff as the left overall unhooked itself. "He's out of his mind. Julian could do worse than a woman like you, pobyd or no. And despite your checkered past, you've really done your best to help. Well, besides tonight, of course."

"I can't figure out how they did it," Lillie said, more to herself than Benetta. "I've replayed the scene over and over again. I kept the cupcakes covered until I plated them. Everyone took one. Rey stood watch while Kathryn and I went outside."

"Have you considered it might not have been added to the cupcakes after the fact? Maybe someone poisoned your flour when you weren't looking."

*Or milk...* Lillie pushed that aside. It felt like a violation to the most intimate degree. "If that's the case, I've got bigger problems than two spoiled events."

"Well, if anyone can figure it out, it's you," Benetta said, rehooking the right clasp on the overalls after it came undone. "But in the meantime, I do apologize, but I won't be eating anything from your store in the next few days."

"You haven't been to my store in weeks," Lillie said.

"Roudie doesn't just bring flowers, you know." She winked at Lillie. "Speaking of, I suppose I should probably get him his clothes back. Or maybe not." A lecherous smile appeared on her face. "I don't mind seeing him in his drawers."

Lillie couldn't help but smile. "I'm glad the two of you have found happiness."

"Me, too." She turned to leave. "Good luck. Let us know when it's safe to come back to the bakery!"

~

The Slooses were closed and their windows were dark when Lillie got back to her side of town. She unlocked the bakery and placed the half-empty box of cupcakes in the back room before coming out to inspect what she still had out on display. Everything here had been baked two days ago, which meant everything here was *presumably* safe to sell. But their freshness was waning, and if Lillie were being honest, it was probably best to toss them. Once the rumor mill got started, she wouldn't have a single customer tomorrow—or the next day, either.

She padded into the kitchen to find her sack of gold and groaned at the light weight. Refunding Mr. Abora was going to hurt. She'd expected ups and downs starting over in a new town, but lately, there seemed more downs than ups.

More concerning, though, was that Lillie no longer felt comfortable baking in her own kitchen—

at least not until Greeley let her know what was making people sick.

"Best not to get bent out of shape yet," Lillie whispered to herself. "Let Greeley find out what it actually is. Then we'll dispose of anything bad."

She groaned, thinking of her sack of gold. She really, *really* hoped it wouldn't come to that, because replenishing all her supplies might cost more than Lillie had.

The thought doused her with cold water. Sure, she'd been in rough patches before—like when her oven had been out of commission—but this seemed a little more than the run-of-the-mill problems. If people didn't trust that her goods were safe to eat, that was a more permanent issue than her oven being out a few days. She'd worked so hard to build trust, and for someone to light a match and burn it down?

And for what? Because Lillie was trying to do the right thing? Because she'd dared catch the eye of Julian Globe?

Tears threatened to fall down her cheeks, and even though she was alone, she refused to let them. She wouldn't go down in defeat because of this. She'd do what she always did, what Bev back at the Weary Dragon had taught her to do. Put on her apron and get to the bottom of things.

There was a soft knock at her back door, and

Lillie quickly wiped her cheeks before rushing over to see who it could be. It was too early for Julian, but perhaps he'd heard... Her pulse quickened at the thought of him coming to her rescue (even though she really didn't need one).

Instead, Nikola stood on her back step, rubbing her hands together nervously.

Lillie's stomach dropped as she mentally calculated the days. Had she forgotten the Kovens' anniversary? "Is everything okay?"

"Yes, fine." She looked nervous anyway. "Just wanted to talk with you about our anniversary surprise."

"Please tell me I didn't forget," Lillie said. "Or that you want to cancel it—"

"No, no, it's tomorrow," Nikola said with a thin smile. "Thankfully. It would've been awful with how sick we've been. Thankfully, Greeley got us sorted. We're both feeling right as rain again. And no extra magical nonsense, either. Have no clue where the fish are around here, and that's how I like it until I get on the water."

Lillie exhaled. She should've told Nikola about her troubles, but she couldn't bear to lose another sale. "I'm glad to hear it. You wanted delivery by tomorrow afternoon, right?"

"Well, that's why I came by. I want to surprise Ursil with it when he wakes up, so I was hoping to get it early in the morning instead of the afternoon. If that's all right. I know you're busy."

Lillie opened her mouth to tell her she wouldn't be busy, that the entire town was going to steer clear of her bakery, but that made her realize there was no way she could bake the Kovens' cake with the ingredients she had in her kitchen. Not until Greeley could test all of it.

But there was *another* option. And goodness knows, Lillie could use a friendly ear and *maybe* a long, drawn-out hug to soothe her troubled heart.

"Lillie?" Nikola prompted.

"I'll have it ready for you first thing in the morning," Lillie said with a firm nod. "Promise."

And in the meantime, she'd finally get to find out what Julian had heard on his side of town.

Knowing it was going to be a long night, Lillie went straight to bed, but she was far too excited to get any rest. She woke at the usual time then quickly dressed in her nicest outfit and checked her reflection as best she could in the dark. There was no helping her wild hair, nor the nervous look in her eye, but somehow, she had a feeling Julian wouldn't mind seeing her in any state. Besides that, she was going to Julian's in the name of romance and providing a lovely surprise for her favorite neighbors.

Even if she ran the risk of running afoul of Mr.

Globe.

Again.

Last time she'd baked with Julian, he'd told her to help herself to everything in his kitchen (though she'd insisted on bringing her own supplies). Today, she was completely at his mercy, and grateful for that, too. It was hard enough to sneak through the dark town empty-handed without being seen by the small folk, including Eldred Talonfoot, an owl friendly with Rey, who'd mentioned he'd seen shadows around the bakery. Lillie was half-convinced the snooty owl was on Mr. Globe's payroll (however that looked to a talking bird).

But for once, nary a soul was stirring in Silverkeep as she strode up to Julian's kitchen door, heart pounding and palms sweating as she knocked. She took a step back, reminding herself that this was for Ursil and Nikola, and for romance, and...well, maybe for herself, too. Tonight had been nothing short of awful, and she desperately needed a kind face and to create something that didn't make anyone sick before she drove herself batty.

There was a noise on the other side, and Lillie held her breath, panic rising in her chest. Was someone there with him? Kathryn had spoken about their long conversations; had she invited herself to Julian's to gather more intelligence on Lillie?

Or worse, in the days between when Julian had

penned his heartfelt letter and now, had Julian's former flame reignited his affections?

She was second-guessing her decision to be here —not only because she might confirm that Julian had moved on, but also *his father* and *her secret*— when the door opened.

"Lils?"

She exhaled a soft breath, her heart melting into a puddle at his wide smile. Every bit of him was perfect, from the way he towered over her, his broad shoulders, his dark brown skin and eyes, and black hair that curled onto his forehead. He shared many features with his father, but his eyes were full of a warmth Audo could never aspire to.

"Hi," Lillie whispered, more because she couldn't find enough air than because she was trying to stay quiet. "Can I come in?"

"I thought we weren't seeing each other," Julian said with a smile that told her he did *not* mind the impromptu visit.

"Erm, I'm sorry if I'm interrupting—"

"Never." Julian stepped back and let her inside. "What's going on?"

"I need to make a dessert," Lillie said. "And I think someone's poisoned my kitchen supplies."

"What?" His brows knitted together. "You're joking."

Lillie filled him in as she bustled around the

kitchen, getting what she needed for the Kovens' cake. Julian, of course, stood to the side and listened intently, the furrow in his brow growing more pronounced as Lillie gave him the full picture—though she couldn't *quite* bring herself to tell him her suspicions about Kathryn yet. Partially because she was afraid of what Julian might say if she brought her up.

He listened silently until she was done then shook his head. "I haven't heard a single thing about it. I've been busy in the bakery, and keeping to myself mostly, but you'd think someone would've mentioned it."

"The fisherfolk were all home yesterday, but I'm sure the rumor mill will get going this morning," Lillie said. "Especially after Mr. Abora's event had the same calamity."

"You think it's something in your bakery?" Julian asked.

"It's looking that way." She poured flour into a bowl. "I don't feel comfortable using my flour or sugar until I know for sure. But the Kovens are such dears to me, and they already paid so..." She gestured to the room. "Here I am."

"Of course," Julian said with a nod. "You said Greeley Sloos can test for the poison?"

"Yes. I'll bring him the remaining cupcakes in the morning." She sighed as she added sugar to an empty bowl. "Julian, I hate this. Someone's clearly trying to ruin my business, and they have no qualms about hurting people to do it. How can someone dislike me that much?"

"Do you have any idea who's behind it?" Julian asked.

She hesitated as she uncorked the jug of milk. Kathryn had clearly staked her claim on Julian, but what Lillie *didn't* know was whether Julian reciprocated. Best to ease her into the conversation and gauge Julian's reaction. "I have some ideas."

"My father?"

She spared him a look before encouraging the butter to churn. "Do you disagree?"

"It's not his style," Julian said. "And he hasn't mentioned anything about wanting you out of business. At least, no more than usual."

"Well, that's comforting." It didn't absolve him though. Mr. Globe had an entire life that Julian didn't know about. But instead of pushing the issue further, Lillie pulled the cocoa powder toward her, scooped some into the dry mixture, and braced herself to ask about Kathryn. Here in this room, with Julian watching her, it was much harder to talk about her—and if Lillie were really being honest with herself, it was because she was afraid of the answer.

*Coward,* she muttered to herself. *Just ask.*

"I hear Kathryn's been in the café a lot," she forced out. It wasn't what she should've asked, but at least Lillie had mentioned her by name and could watch Julian's reaction.

"I can't say I mind the extra business, but I could do without listening to the same stump speech from Clancy," Julian said, giving no hint that he minded who came with the stump speech—or that he had any inkling that Kathryn was the mastermind behind the poisonings. "He can get through it now without stumbling over it. But then again, I've heard it so many times, I can probably recite it for him."

Lillie forced a smile, still unable to ask the questions she really wanted to ask. *Are you and Kathryn together again? Do you still miss me like you said in your letter?*

Instead, she blurted, "Wineke's still working on her speech."

That seemed news to Julian. "Wineke's running?"

"You didn't know?" Lillie bit her lip. That wasn't good news for her apothecary neighbor.

"No, all I heard about were Kemp and Clancy," Julian said. "But that's great. I think she'd do a good job. She's certainly stubborn enough to get things done."

"You really didn't hear that she's running?" Lillie

asked. "At all?"

"No, but I wouldn't worry about that. I've been keeping my head down and not talking to anyone lately," he said with a shrug. "Clancy's stump speeches here mean we're busier than ever, so I barely have time to think while we're open. Everyone else around here might've known." He brightened. "But I do know who I'm voting for."

"I'm sure Kathryn would have something to say about it if you vote against her candidate," Lillie said, watching his reaction closely again.

"Votes are private, and she'll be moving on after the election," Julian replied casually, as if they were discussing the weather.

That gave Lillie some hope that perhaps Kathryn's attempts to seduce him weren't going as well as she hoped...and also brought into stark relief that *if* Kathryn were the poisoner, she probably wouldn't tell Julian about it.

Julian nodded toward the two bowls over her shoulder. "Are you missing any ingredients?"

"No. Why?"

"You stopped assembling the cake, so I was wondering." He smiled. "Not that I mind talking with you, but—"

"Ah, well." She cleared her throat, a blush rising to her cheeks. "Unfortunately, I'm going to have to...ask you to leave the room for a little while."

He frowned. "What do you mean? Do you have some kind of secret recipe for your chocolate cake you don't want me to steal?"

"No, it's not that." She exhaled, willing the blush to stay off her cheeks. "Nikola asked me to... make their cake special."

"Make it special how? Extra chocolate?" He tilted his head, his eyes alight with interest and amusement.

"Magic," Lillie said, her face growing warmer by the second. "She wants me to infuse it with an extra bit of...love." She swallowed hard. "You know, with my pobyd magic."

"Like the mind-control cookies?" Julian asked with a teasing smile.

She glared at him. "They were an *encouragement* to tell the truth. And this is an *encouragement to...*"

"To what?" Julian's brows wagged.

"It probably wouldn't be for the best to have you in here while I'm making the batter. There will be lots of...feelings floating around. It tends to spread, you know." She crossed her arms over her chest. "And since we're not supposed to be speaking to each other..."

"Mm. Is that why you never responded to my letter?"

Lillie's heart skipped. "I've been...busy. With my bakery being sabotaged and all." *Possibly by your ex-girlfriend. Or current girlfriend.* "But as soon as I figure that out—"

"You could always respond now."

Lillie wanted to—oh, how she wanted to—but something held her back. Whether it was because Kathryn had gotten under her skin, or because she needed to get a move on so she could be out of his bakery before anyone else woke up, or even her own cowardice... Lillie shook her head.

"I need to get this done," she whispered.

Julian took a step back, hurt flashing across his face. "Well, I can understand that. Last time we baked together, Zena Plotter got a mushroom in her shop." He thumbed toward the oven. "I just put in a batch of cookies. Do you think those will be influenced by your...well, influence?"

"No, they shouldn't be," Lillie said, grateful they could talk about something other than the elephant in the room. "I'll be sure to pull them out when they're ready."

"Great." He took a step back. "Well, I'll leave you to it."

He started walking toward the back door when Lillie called his name. "I just... Thank you. I really am grateful that you're being so accommodating. You're a wonderful friend to me."

"Of course." Was that more hurt? Lillie tried to ignore it. "Let me know when it's safe to come back."

It took Lillie a few minutes to shake off the lingering unease from talking with Julian. She'd hoped for… Well, she wasn't sure what she'd been hoping for. At a minimum, unspoiled ingredients and a working oven. But the awkward conversation between them wasn't satisfactory, either. She'd wanted him to adamantly deny there was *anything* happening between him and Kathryn, and his nonchalance was more upsetting than anything.

Then again, she hadn't even asked him outright. *Coward.*

"I'm wasting time," she muttered, staring at the two bowls before her. "Focus, Lillie." She bent down so her face was level with the two bowls. "Listen up. I need you to be the most delicious cake in the history of cakes, but you also need to be…well, you need to be filled with love. Bursting with affection and appreciation and…"

Julian's face flashed in her mind, and a pang of discomfort rang through her. It seemed like a chasm had opened between them. She pushed all the uncertainty Kathryn had planted aside and instead recited his love-filled letter from memory.

Affection blossomed in her chest as she fell victim to her own magic. A goofy smile spread across her face and, full of love and all kinds of butterflies, she set to combining her wet and dry ingredients then poured the combined mixture into the two floured pans. As she worked, she daydreamed about all those beautiful moments with Julian. How he *always* seemed delighted to see her. How he'd let her inside without a second thought. How he'd vacated his kitchen in the middle of his prime baking time because *Lillie* was desperate. She thought about him paying for her oven repair and how amazing it was to work in proximity to each other. How it had felt to be carried out of the Silverkeep Inn, to know even in her dazed mind that she was safe with him. That he would never *ever* let her down.

The idea that this man would have eyes for anyone else was absolutely ridiculous.

He'd offered to give up his bakery so they could be together. She'd known that would break him as much as it would break her, so instead they were just…not together. He'd promised to wait until Lillie had enough gold to pay off his father so he could no longer meddle in their love lives.

Or, until Lillie told him the truth about what she'd done in Lower Pigsend.

A tear leaked down her cheek before she could stop it, and she gasped when a fingertip brushed it away. She opened her eyes to find Julian standing next to her, affection shimmering in his gaze. She licked her lips. She should've probably stepped away—and definitely should've told him to leave this love-infested room.

But instead, she grabbed him by the shirt, pulling him down, and smashed her lips to his.

Where kissing was concerned, Lillie didn't have the most experience, but there was enough magic and pent-up energy in the air that she honestly didn't care. He tasted like coffee and *him,* and his lips were just as soft as she'd hoped they'd be. He wrapped his arms around her, holding her tightly and securely, as if she'd break if he let her go. She was swept away by the sensation of him, content to never come down from this incredible height of happiness.

And yet, something niggled in the back of her mind.

Something about how he wasn't supposed to be in here. Something about this cake that had overcome her love and affection. Something about....

Her eyes snapped open as the weight of what she was doing crashed into her. She pushed Julian away roughly, but he didn't go very far because he was pressed against his table. She stared at him, heavy-lidded, lips swollen, knowing he was quite drunk on the love magic she'd infused into the cake.

The same way *she* was drunk on her own magic.

And yet, the feeling of his lips echoed on hers. She wanted *more.*

He took a step toward her, tilting his mouth toward hers, and it was truly the most painful thing she'd ever done to turn away. Wordlessly, she dragged him out into the backyard, where the fresh air would clear the magic from his mind. As soon as the cold hit her cheeks, she sobered up—and one look at Julian's wide-eyed, shocked stare told her he had as well.

"What…happened…?" he stammered.

"That's why I told you to stay out of the kitchen," Lillie said, unable to meet his gaze. "When I'm infusing a pastry with a little something extra, I let it all out in the kitchen. And it can feel… overwhelming." She swallowed hard. "I'm sorry."

"You're sorry? I'm sorry!" He rubbed his mouth. "I never would've— Lillie, I feel like…" He shook his head. "That was a mistake."

Something uncomfortable slipped down Lillie's stomach. "I see."

He blinked, turning to her with his mouth open. "Wait. I don't mean— That's not what I—"

"No, I understand," Lillie forced out. "You've got other interests at the moment. It's fine. Probably better that we don't speak of this again." She straightened her shoulders despite everything in her shattering like glass. "I'm going to finish my cake.

Then I'll be out of your hair. I'll leave the door open so the…magic can dissipate, and you won't have any further trouble."

"Lillie, wait—" Julian started, but Lillie pushed his hand away.

"Please, you don't have to explain yourself further. It was a mistake, as you said," Lillie said, forcing a smile. "Just a byproduct of the magic. I understand. You should probably leave me until I'm finished. I'll be sure to clean up on my way out."

He went to follow her, and she held up her hand.

"Don't. Just…" She swallowed. "Just don't."

It was hard enough to stomach that Julian hadn't wanted to kiss her, but to walk back into the kitchen where things had happened, to be smacked in the face with the love magic, was rubbing salt in her already wounded heart. But instead of drumming up all the affectionate feelings, the magic brought tears to her eyes that she struggled to wipe away. Thankfully, the cakes were already in the oven and the buttercream sat in a bag, waiting to be piped, so she wasn't in danger of letting her morose energy leak into the baked goods.

The only thing that kept her from falling into a

large pit of despair was the scent of chocolate wafting by her nose. One could never be too upset when chocolate cakes were baking—though as the moments slogged by like molasses, she began to think that perhaps even chocolate cake wasn't enough to dispel the pain lodged in her chest.

She decided she wouldn't take up more of Julian's time or kitchen, so as soon as the cakes were done, she yanked the tins out, wrapped them in towels, and gathered the two pastry bags of chocolate buttercream, whispering to them that they should stay cool despite the warm cakes. Then, she piled up the two tins and bags as best she could and sauntered outside, ready to face Julian again and hear his explanation.

But he wasn't there.

She swallowed, looking around for where he might've run off to, and refused to let herself get swept away by the sadness. The buttercream could still be influenced, and Lillie was bound and determined to deliver a cake full of *love* to the Kovens, not one laced with heartbreaking disappointment.

"Thank you again," Lillie called to no one. "I'm done."

She walked back to the bakery with her chin held high, let herself in the back door with some difficulty. The cakes were ready to decorate, so Lillie got to work, adding a crumb layer before slathering on a thicker layer of chocolate buttercream. She lost herself in the decorations, piping small rosettes along the bottom of the platter and using her spatula to create waves in the thick frosting. When she was finished, she spun the cake around, pleased with herself. She dipped her finger into the buttercream and took a taste.

Affection bloomed in her chest, and she *almost* forgot why she was mad at Julian in the first place.

"Perfect," she said, picking up the platter and walking upstairs.

"You're the best," Nikola whispered, gently taking the cake from her. "Ursil's going to be over the moon."

"I baked it at Julian Globe's bakery," Lillie said. "Just to be on the safe side."

"What do you mean?" Nikola asked with a frown. "Don't tell me more people have gotten sick."

"Don't trouble yourself with it," Lillie said. "I'm only telling you in case you hear something today. But I took every single precaution necessary—including Julian's ingredients."

Nikola smirked. "I'm sure that was absolutely awful for you. Not as if you two haven't been mooning over each other for the past few weeks."

The magic that had buoyed Lillie's mood

popped like a bubble, leaving the cold reality of what had actually happened in its wake. Tears threatened at the corners of her eyes, and she swallowed hard to keep them where they should be. "I'm so happy I could do this for you two. I hope it's everything you were hoping for. I put as much love as I possibly could into it. Happy anniversary and congratulations."

Nikola thanked her and quietly shut the door, and Lillie meandered down to the bakery, her broken heart aching as she unlocked the door and stood amongst the flour, sugar, and other supplies that she no longer felt safe baking with. This morning had been a one-two punch, and Lillie wasn't sure how much more she could take.

She'd manage to stave off the worst of it while icing and decorating the cake, but left with nothing but her thoughts, she fell headfirst into the memory of the most earth-shattering and *embarrassing* kiss of her life. If she could've frozen time and lived in that moment, she would've been happy for years. But then Julian had to go and ruin it with his big mouth.

*"That was a mistake."*

Alone in her bakery and knowing no one else would be around to interrupt her for a few hours, Lillie finally let the tears drip down her cheeks.

"It's for the best," she whispered to herself.

"Now, you don't have to worry about paying Mr. Globe back so quickly. You can weather a few more storms—including this one. And you won't provoke him anymore by making eyes at his son against his wishes."

Her gaze kept flitting to the door, hoping Julian would come barging in any minute now. She imagined him sweeping her into an embrace, swearing it had been a mistake to say it was a mistake. Then he'd kiss her again, and she'd forgive him, and they'd go along their merry way.

But the minutes passed by and no one came to the door, leaving her with a dull echo in her chest, like someone had taken her heart out and left a hole behind.

"Suppose Kathryn was right. He does have better options now," Lillie muttered, running her finger along the wood grain on her table. She, of course, thought she and Julian were a far better match than the overwhelming campaign manager, but perhaps she didn't know Julian as well as she'd thought.

And how could she? All they had were stolen moments in a kitchen, early morning baking sessions, and the occasional conversation about his father. They'd never actually spent time getting to know one another. Perhaps she had the measure of him completely wrong.

The letter he'd written her was stale now. As if that version of Julian was a stranger who'd strung her along until something better appeared.

She found his letter and ripped it up, throwing it outside in the compost pile.

With nothing to do but dwell on her own sadness, Lillie remained in her pity party for longer than was probably acceptable. When a soft knock broke her reverie, her hopes shot to the sky. But as soon as she flung open the door, they were dashed just as quickly.

"H-hi." Esmerelda Honeygood stood on her back step, her wagon laden with milk and eggs behind her. "Erm. Good morning, that is. I'm here with your delivery."

"I thought you said you didn't want to deliver to me," Lillie said, not caring that she sounded a little catty. "That if I wanted the concierge—"

"I changed my mind," Esmerelda said pointedly.

"Why?"

"Does it matter?" she replied with a huff. "Do you want to barter or not?"

"I…do, but…" Lillie looked back at her bakery, with supplies she wasn't sure she could use. "I'm sorry, Esmerelda. The bakery's closed. I can't purchase anything from you today. Someone's trying to sabotage me."

Esmerelda's mouth dropped open. "What?

Who'd want to do that?"

"I have a few guesses," Lillie said with a sigh. "But I can't bake anything until I know that what I've got here isn't...well, *poisoned* for lack of a better word." She glanced toward the cupcakes off to the side. "Greeley Sloos is taking a look at them today. Hopefully, he'll have answers for me, and I can get back to work soon."

"Goodness gracious," Esmerelda said, looking genuinely upset. "That's awful. I'm so sorry."

"I'll survive, I think," Lillie said gravely.

Esmerelda swallowed. "Do you think you could at least make me some butter to sell? Not that..." Her face reddened. "Things haven't been so great for us, either. The butter is a rather large part of our income, it seems, and—"

"Oh, of course," Lillie said with a smile she barely felt.

Esmerelda brought three jugs inside for Lillie to whip into shape, but as Lillie poured the first one into the bowl, she couldn't help second-guessing herself. Had someone lined the bowls with some kind of poison? Was she inadvertently sending bad butter to the Honeygolds? What would that do to their business?

"Is something supposed to be happening?" Esmerelda asked.

Lillie glanced down at the milk that was

stagnant. "Sorry, lost in thought." She shook her head to clear the thoughts from it. "Okay, please churn."

The milk cooperated, and Lillie forced herself to think of nothing more than butter solids coagulating into a mass in the center. She repeated that process another two times, although once or twice her mind got away from her.

"Thank you for this. Butter churning isn't the most fun of activities, and with Kristin's leg..."

"How is she?" Lillie asked.

"She's going stir crazy, to be honest. She's read every book we own and wants me to travel to the nearest bookstore to buy her more. Apparently, the Silverkeep library doesn't carry enough interesting titles for her satisfaction."

"I bet." A bookstore had opened in Silverkeep, but considering they only kept magical tomes, Lillie didn't want to mention that to Esmerelda. Perhaps Lillie could make a trip up to see Kristin. It would be better than wallowing in her own sadness.

"Sorry," Esmerelda said quietly. "I didn't mean to burden you with our troubles when you've got some of your own."

"Helping other people usually makes me forget about mine," Lillie said as the butter finished separating in the bowls. "If you need more, don't hesitate to ask. I get a bit stir crazy if I can't use my magic regularly."

Esmerelda nodded. "Assuming everyone's back today, this should be plenty. Is…." She tilted her head at Lillie. "*Is* everyone back at the wharf market today?"

"They should be," Lillie said with a thin smile. Only a handful of sailors had consumed her pastries last night, so everyone else would be fine. "I'm glad you came by. I hope we can be friends, Esmerelda."

The dairy farmer flinched before she could stop herself. "Yes, well. Not sure about that. But I'm willing to consider a business arrangement in the meantime."

*Small steps.* "Whatever you like. Good luck today."

~

After Esmerelda took her leave, Lillie tidied her kitchen and front room, but it was still clean from when her oven was out, so she was very quickly without anything to do. She was too embarrassed to check on Reginald and Haruko, but Haruko's glassblowing shop across the way was still closed anyway. Not a great sign, but at least nothing was on fire.

Thankfully, there was finally movement in the apothecary shop, and Lillie gathered the box of cupcakes and headed over. Greeley was in the front room with Fawn, talking about their plans for the day, and both turned when Lillie walked through the door.

"Oh, no." Greeley straightened. "Don't tell me..."

Lillie gave them the full story, including how very sure she was that no one had been able to put anything on the cupcakes before they'd been eaten. Greeley and Fawn listened with matching intense stares before turning to each other and tossing out theories.

"Something in the cupcakes, then?" Fawn muttered.

"That's what I'm thinking. Or maybe someone sprayed the air," Greeley replied. "Perhaps we're looking at an aerosol—"

"Then there wouldn't have been anyone in the room who wasn't unaffected," Fawn replied. "And Lillie—"

"Yes, Lillie." Greeley turned to her. "Did you taste your own cupcakes? Any ill effects?"

"I did, and to my knowledge, I didn't experience anything out of the ordinary," she said. "I tasted everything as I went, too. Nothing seemed wrong with them."

If Lillie thought that might've stumped the apothecaries, she was mistaken.

"That does make it interesting," Greeley said to Fawn. "We were thinking the poison might be resistant to pobyds."

"Are pobyds immune to a lot of poisons?" Lillie asked.

"Oh, yes," Fawn said with an emphatic nod. "Much like you can handle hot pans and encourage deliciousness, there are some poisons that don't affect you like they would someone else. We had a hunch—especially if it turned out that the pastries were the problem—that we were looking at something in that category, so I started assembling a list of the more common ones."

"I don't know if I like the sound of that," Lillie said with a frown. "That sounds almost... intentional. Like they knew they could slip it past me and make everyone sick."

"We'll get to the bottom of it. Tom's already spent some time at the magical bookstore, too. Clark said he would rush order some particular books in, but it may be a day or two," Greeley said. "First thing, now that we've got a few samples, we'll be able to figure out what it is. Then we can move on to figuring out where it came from."

Lillie exhaled. As bad as the night before had been, at least there was *some* hope on the horizon. "Not that I'm rushing you, but how long is this going to take?"

"The experiments themselves can take upwards of an hour, and that's assuming they work," Greeley said. "Sometimes they'll sit and nothing will happen. It's a process of elimination at this point, unfortunately."

She considered the cupcake, which looked quite innocent for all the trouble it had caused. "Is there a way you could let me know which ingredient is the problem?"

"That's going to be hard in a baked cupcake," Fawn said. "Everything's all mixed together. But once we identify the poison, we can test each ingredient separately."

"Don't worry, Lillie. We'll sort this out," Fawn said. "Keep your chin up."

Easier said than done. "Thanks. Keep me posted."

With nothing else to do, Lillie took herself for a long walk down the beach, which she'd hoped would clear her mind, but all it did was remind her of Julian calling their kiss a mistake. She'd have to return his bowls, which meant she'd have to face him eventually.

And Kathryn.

She kicked a shell into the ocean.

Although she would've rather kept walking until she reached the next town over, Lillie turned and walked back to Silverkeep. Greeley had said it would be a few hours, but she was impatient and made a beeline for the apothecary anyway, finding Wineke manning the front desk. She waved at Lillie absentmindedly, muttering to herself as she leafed through a stack of cards.

"Is Greeley back there?" Lillie asked.

Wineke nodded, barely looking up.

"Wineke?"

"Sorry, trying to prepare for tonight," she said, picking up a charcoal and scribbling something else. "I'm not that great at public speaking, and I'm really nervous." She finally put down the cards. "No news yet on the cupcakes. I know they've got at least ten tests in progress right now. If and when I hear something, I'll let you know." She returned to the cards. "But right now, I'm freaking out about tonight, so if you want to talk with them, you can go back there."

Lillie considered her friend, a pang of guilt echoing in her chest. She'd been so concerned with the Fisherfolk Council and poisoning, she hadn't really helped her with her campaign, except for a few conversations here and there. "Why don't you practice with me? It's not as if I have anything else to do this morning."

"Oh, really?" Wineke's face lit up with happiness and relief. "You mean it? Greeley, well, he's wonderful at so many things, but once he gets an idea in his mind, he's going to be chewing on it until he's done—and these cupcakes are a puzzle."

"Show me what you've got."

Wineke exhaled and laid out her speech for Lillie to see. "I've got five minutes to convince the fisherfolk to vote for me, and I can't get the timing right on any of it. This one section." She pointed to a card that had several strikethroughs on it. "And when I'm mayor, I will ensure that every single person... Every single...citizen. Every citizen." She let out a breath. "Public speaking is *not* my bailiwick. And I can't figure out the best way to phrase this. And..." She sighed. "I don't know. Maybe I'm in over my head. I should pull out of the race, shouldn't I?"

"Absolutely not," Lillie said with a meaningful smile. "You know, Rey should be up soon looking for his pastry. He's got enough confidence for both of us, and he'll absolutely be able to wordsmith this to something great."

~

As predicted, when Lillie popped over to the bakery to find him, Rey was more than enthusiastic about helping Wineke, professing that he'd taken no fewer than three classes on public speaking at Silverkeep University.

"You were enrolled at the university?" Wineke asked dubiously as she flipped the apothecary's sign to closed so they wouldn't be interrupted.

"Well, not *technically* enrolled, but I've got half a mind to write them and take their exams so I can get my diploma," Rey said, adjusting his tunic. "The point is, I know public speaking. I'm more than happy to assist you in getting this speech in perfect shape. Now." He came to the edge of the counter. "Shoulders back. Chin up. You need to project authority if you're going to win these fisherfolk over. Now. Charm me!"

Wineke held her cards aloft and opened her mouth to speak, but Rey made a hissing sound.

"No, no, no. You've got to have it *memorized*! You aren't going to impress a single soul by reading off cards, you know—I bet you that Clancy Cast has his stump speech memorized."

"Yep," Lillie muttered, pushing Julian from her mind. "He's been doing it every day at Globe Café."

"I don't think I can memorize this," Wineke said with a frown. "It's a lot—"

"It's just five minutes. You can do five minutes." Rey began pacing like a teacher in front of a college class. "You don't want to trip over your words. You want them to fall out of your mouth as if you've said them a million times—because you have!"

"I don't know if I have time for that much practice," Wineke said.

"Especially because you keep changing the words," Lillie added with a knowing smile.

"First things first, we need to finalize the speech then," Rey said. "Let's see what we've got to work with."

Wineke did her best to lay out all the cards so Rey could inspect the speech. He muttered to himself as he read, pointing out changes to phrases and words he wanted Wineke to make. "Yes, let's make this section stronger," he said, pointing to the section where Wineke was talking about Mr. Globe. "We should be more vociferous in our anger toward Mr. Globe. He's not very popular at the moment, even up in the nonmagical part of town. The more we hammer on him, the better we'll be."

"I agree with that," Lillie said. "But we probably shouldn't call him a monster. Perhaps 'not looking out for our best interests.' That might resonate better with the fisherfolk. They don't love Mr. Globe, but I don't think they'd go for besmirching his character outright like that."

"I should've asked Nikola and Ursil to help," Wineke said, scribbling through that sentence and rewriting it. "Do you think they're available?"

"Ah, well, I stopped in earlier today," Rey said. "Wanted to wish them a happy anniversary. They were *very* busy staring into each other's eyes while eating a chocolate cake. Was that your doing, Lillie?"

Lillie couldn't help but grin. "Yes. I had to make

it at Julian's last night, but—"

"Oh, you did?" Wineke asked with a smirk.

"Because the entirety of my kitchen is suspect, and I'd never forgive myself if I sold them something that made them sick." Lillie paused. "Again."

Wineke shifted like she knew something, and Lillie cleared her throat loudly.

"*Back to the matter at hand*, Nikola and Ursil are indisposed for the day. But I can tell you what I know about the fisherfolk, from what I've overheard in the bakery." She pointed at the next line, which continued to talk about Mr. Globe's lack of character. "They probably won't like this, either."

Wineke scowled as she scratched that out, too. "What do you know about the other guy running for the council—Jarvis?"

"Well, he's clearly in Mr. Globe's pocket," Rey said. "Considering…"

"Considering," Lillie said with a knowing nod. "So I don't think you're getting his endorsement. You're really better off trying to get the McTavishes to endorse your campaign."

"I haven't had a chance to meet them yet," Wineke said. "What do you know about them?"

Lillie conveyed all she could—minus the part about Jan's fairy wings—and anything she thought might help Wineke craft her speech. "They're not quite as anti-magic as feared, but they aren't as comfortable with it as other people are. I think if you talk about how you'll ally yourselves with them against Mr. Globe, that might resonate really well."

"Do you think they're going to win?" Wineke asked.

Lillie sat back. "I honestly don't know. Kathryn seems to have convinced Jarvis and Clancy that she's got the election in the bag, whatever that means." Her gaze drifted back to the curtain, where Greeley and Fawn were running tests. Was part of her plan to sabotage Lillie, or was that an added bonus? "Between you, me, and the trees, I wouldn't put it past her to be behind all this poisoning."

"That doesn't surprise me in the least," Rey said. "I got a bad feeling about her from the moment I met her. She's all but taken over the Silverkeep Inn in the evenings, and she's downright awful to listen to. Yet all the people at the Silverkeep Inn seem to be willing to vote for Clancy."

Wineke sucked in a breath. "That's not good."

"You probably weren't going to win those folks anyway," Lillie said. "They're all transplants, remember? You've got to focus on the fisherfolk. Those are really the ones who're going to decide this election."

"Besides that," Rey said. "I bet you two chocolate chip cookies that half the people in the northern part of town are going to *say* they'll vote for Clancy but end up voting for someone else. I don't know a single person who wants to give Mr. Globe more power."

"I agree with that," Wineke said. "Okay. I think we've revised this to within an inch of its life. Why don't I rewrite it? Then we can practice until I've got it memorized."

~

The morning turned to afternoon, and the practice session only halted when Wineke announced that she was hungry. Since Lillie had nothing to offer that she was comfortable selling, they ventured down to the fisherfolk market in search of something to eat.

"Because I wouldn't be caught *dead* buying anything from Julian Globe," Wineke said.

Lillie attempted to hide the flinch, but unfortunately, Wineke was quite perceptive.

"What's up?" She nudged Lillie. "That was a grimace, not a lovesick sigh. And you were acting weird about baking with him, too."

Lillie really, *really* didn't want Wineke to know the whole truth, but she also really needed to talk with someone about it. She considered which bits of the truth she was comfortable sharing—and which parts she definitely wanted to keep to herself.

"Long story short, I think he's decided he

doesn't like me anymore." She glanced around, making sure no one was listening as they walked toward the market. "Kathryn's his ex-girlfriend."

"*No!*" Wineke's voice carried so far, a flock of seagulls were spooked.

"Ssh!" Lillie shook her head. "In any case, he made it clear to me last night that he's no longer interested."

Wineke pursed her lips. "I don't believe that for a second."

"What?"

"That he's not into you. The man was barely able to form words when he brought you breakfast after he *rescued you* from a destroyed building." Wineke shook her head. "No, something else is going on. Did you talk to him about whatever happened?"

"I think it's possible we misread him," Lillie murmured. "Kathryn's much prettier and...well, she and Julian have clearly rekindled their old flame."

"Or, that Kathryn is trying to get into your head," Wineke said. "You think she's behind the poisoning, too, don't you? Maybe she's trying to distract you so you won't suspect her."

"I think getting Julian is a bonus," Lillie said. "Currently, my theory is she's trying to snatch two dragon eggs in one theft. Get her candidates in office and run me out of town."

"What are you gonna do about it? Tell Juno?"

"I don't know. Nothing until we know what's making everyone sick, that's for sure." She sighed as they arrived at the market. "It's for the best. I don't need to be tangled up in more drama with the Globes."

"Look, I'm not saying that's what's going on, but if Julian picks her over you, he's an idiot," Wineke said. "You're smart, you've got the biggest heart I've ever seen, and if you don't mind my saying so, you're flat-out gorgeous. Way better than some political consultant."

Lillie flushed. "Thanks, Wineke."

While Lillie frequented the market nearly every day for produce, she'd never stopped at any of the food booths. A cornucopia of options awaited, including steamed shellfish and vegetable stew, fall corn cooked over a grill, and lots and *lots* of fish. Wineke was clearly the expert at finding a good meal and hemmed and hawed over the selection until she finally picked grilled fish sandwiches for them both.

"Do you bake the bread yourself?" Lillie asked the vendor, who she hadn't ever spoken to before.

"Indeed." He eyed her. "And no, I don't want to buy from you. I'm still not right after eating your pastry the other night." He grunted. "Hope you ain't bringing anything to the meeting tonight."

Lillie's face fell, but Wineke spoke up for her. "If you have any information about who's poisoning Lillie's pastries, do come out with it. Because my partner and his assistant are currently piecing together what made everyone sick, and—"

"It's fine, Wineke," Lillie said, paying the man a silver for her meal, as she wanted to get out of the conversation.

Wineke pouted as they meandered back toward the apothecary, and Lillie picked at the meal. The fish was flaky and buttery—not to mention spiced well—but the bread was underbaked and gummy.

"I think you should sell to him, when you're back to baking again," Wineke said, making a face. "He can't hold one bad night against you, can he?"

It seemed he could, and he wasn't the only one. As Lillie looked around, it became clear that none of the wharf market folks wanted to talk with her. Even Eduardo, her sugar merchant, looked the other way as she walked by. Had she really fallen so far from grace?

"Look, I have another favor to ask you," Wineke said. "A big one."

"Anything." Especially since Wineke was her only friend right now.

"Could you…come with me tonight? For moral support?"

"I don't know if you want me there, Wineke," Lillie said. "It's clear no one's really happy with me, thanks to the last Fisherfolk Council meeting."

"They will be when Greeley figures out what's made everyone sick," Wineke said. "And we find out who's responsible and send them off to a prison in King's Capital."

"That's going to be a large hill to climb between now and this evening," Lillie said.

"Okay, fine, but you aren't going to give them the satisfaction of seeing you bury your head in the sand either, are you?" Wineke asked. "If anything, it'll prove to this dastardly culprit that you aren't to be messed with."

"Then they might try even harder," Lillie said.

"But you're not baking anything. What else can they do?"

Lillie considered that point. She did want to show whoever had it in for her that she wasn't to be trifled with. And there was a very good chance, considering Clancy would also be giving a speech like Wineke, that Kathryn would be there. Lillie could spend the rest of the afternoon getting spiffed up and walk into the Fisherfolk Council with her head held high.

"You know what? You're right."

"I'm always right," Wineke said with a smirk.

"But, I mean, Greeley's going to come too,

right?" Lillie said. "He's your partner."

She shrugged. "How much have you seen of him today? I told you, when he gets a project, he doesn't want to rest until it's finished." She shook her head. "It's fine. I know who I'm with."

"Surely, he understands that this is important to you," Lillie said.

Wineke waved her off. "He does. And he'll support me in his own way." She brightened, as if trying her best to ignore her own disappointment. "Shall we take another whack at this speech?"

They practiced and practiced—and practiced more with Rey—until finally, it was time to leave for the Sad Hill. Lillie wasn't sure about her decision to accompany Wineke, even though Rey agreed that Lillie had nothing to be ashamed of, but went along anyway.

But as they walked into the room and every eye landed on her, she would've rather melted into the floor. She took a seat in the back while Wineke conferred with Mr. Abora on the details of the event. Rey had disappeared off her shoulder, and she stared at the door, wondering if Wineke would notice if she snuck out.

"Oh, wow. I'm shocked you showed your face tonight, Lils."

Lillie started as Kathryn sat in the chair in front of her, once again dressed to kill, her dark hair perfectly curled around her face and her lips a devilish shade of red.

Lillie was too startled to respond other than to stammer incredulously.

"I mean, everyone's pretty convinced you poisoned them," she continued. "To the point where the McClarens—"

"McTavishes," Lillie corrected before she could stop herself.

"It doesn't matter." She grinned. "Anyway, they've been distancing themselves from you. I'm surprised they didn't ban you from the event, but maybe they thought you were smarter than that."

"I've done nothing wrong," Lillie said. "And I'll thank you to stop spreading rumors to disrupt my business."

"I don't need to spread anything, Lils. They're doing it all on their own." She glanced at a nearby table—and Lillie was shocked to see a platter of cookies and tartlets. "Don't worry, Julian Globe made all the pastries tonight, so you know they're safe to consume." She winked at Hipolita, who was walking through the door. "Well, I suppose I've got to earn my gold, hm? Good chatting with you, Lils."

Lillie seethed as Kathryn stood and started all but shoving people over to the table. There was a tug at her skirt as Rey climbed back up to stand on her knee.

"I say, that Kathryn woman is awful," Rey said, shaking his head in her direction.

"Rey…" Lillie said mildly. "Do you have… crumbs around your whiskers?"

He turned to her, aghast. "I mean… You can't expect me to… And they look *so* scrumptious…." He bristled and made an attempt to clean his snout. "It was *one* cookie, Lillie. And I daresay that Julian must've learned a thing or two from you because they were as delicious as yours—"

She glared at him.

"I mean not *as* delicious, of course. Missing that exquisite pobyd magic, but—" He chuckled as Lillie's scowl deepened. "I'll just…keep my thoughts to myself."

Lillie sat back, glaring at the table of pastries. She should've been happy that Julian had gotten some business, should've been beaming with pride that he'd improved so much that everyone had something nice to say about his cookies. From this distance, they were well-shaped, well-mixed, and had that perfect mix of crunchy and soft. All of that should've made her happy.

Except that it was *her* customers munching away, murmuring to themselves about how they'd have to give Globe Café another chance, now that Julian Globe had learned to bake.

It was hard not to turn her ire onto Kathryn, whose grating voice carried from across the room. She was practically slapping the cookies into everyone's hands—not caring if they wanted one or not—even Ursil and Nikola, who were the last to arrive. Lillie couldn't help exhaling with relief that they were happy and hale; she hadn't seen them all day, and had been nervous after icing the cake in her bakery.

They settled in beside her, hands intertwined, and stared lovingly at each other until Rey cleared his throat. "Had a good anniversary, did you?"

"Oh, Lillie." Ursil finally broke off from staring at his wife and yanked the pobyd into a hug. "Thank you *so* much for that delicious surprise! You and Nik, I tell ya. I'm blessed to have you in my life."

Affection swooped through Lillie, and she grew a little misty-eyed. "I really needed that today, Ursil. Thank you."

"Did you make those?" Nikola asked, eyeing the cookies on the table.

"No, Kathryn commissioned them from Julian," Lillie said, hoping to sound as neutral as possible. "My bakery is closed at the moment."

"Hah!" Jarvis laughed behind them. "Told ya. Poisoned pastries. Glad I never ate there."

"I know for a fact you've eaten there at least once," Hipolita said, glaring at him from the other side of Lillie. "Because you went with me. But it really… Goodness, the problem was your pastries?"

"It wasn't intentional," Lillie said quickly. "Someone—I'm not naming names—seems to be out to sabotage me. It's some kind of pobyd-resistant poison, or so Greeley thinks." She looked around. "Where is he, anyway? It's about time for the speeches to start."

"Probably still working in the back room with Fawn," Rey said. "I tried to remind them it was time, but…"

"Right, well, suppose we should get started, eh?" Jan McTavish said, coming to stand at the front of the room. "I want to thank everyone for coming tonight, and to…" They spotted Lillie and looked away. "And to apologize for the mishap at the last meeting."

"Mishap? Is that what we're calling it?" Kathryn barked a laugh. "More like intentional poisoning."

"You'll have your time to talk, Ms. Harkness," Orxan said darkly. "But first, we're going to hear from the candidates themselves. After which, we'll ask them to leave so we can conduct our business that was interrupted the other day. The final endorsements will happen at the mayoral election tomorrow evening, and that's when we'll have our vote as well." He cleared his throat. "Which of the candidates would like to go first?"

"I would," Wineke said, stepping forward. "If… I mean, if that's all right."

Mr. Abora and Clancy didn't argue, so Wineke walked to the front of the room. Lillie glanced at the back door, willing Greeley to come. Surely, he wouldn't miss this, would he?

"Good evening," Wineke said. "My name is Wineke Sloos. Some of you might know me as the magical apothecary in Silverkeep. I've decided to throw my hat into the ring for mayor because I feel we need better representation in the town hall."

"Do we, though?" Kathryn said, looking at her nails. "And what does an apothecary know about running a town?"

Wineke opened and closed her mouth, a blush rising up her cheeks. Lillie once again glanced at the door. *Come on, Greeley. Don't miss this. Please.*

"Erm, that is…" Wineke's face was quickly growing redder by the moment. Rey began pantomiming on Lillie's knee, but Wineke was looking everywhere but at him.

Then the back door opened. Greeley slid through, flushed and panting like he'd run there. He gave Wineke a thumbs-up, and she visibly relaxed.

"Right, where was I?" Wineke said, finally spotting Rey. He pantomimed something, and she nodded. "Ah, yes. I know things have been in an upheaval since the queen was dethroned. Trust me that we're not where I thought we'd be, but honestly..." She smiled at Lillie. "I'm starting to think our new location is actually better than our old spot."

"Hear, hear," Mr. Abora said, earning a scowl from everyone.

"I do think, though, that it's time to shake things up—really," Wineke said. "It's obvious that Clancy is going to be in Mr. Globe's pocket—"

"Booo!" came the chorus from the crowd. Lillie snuck a peek at Kathryn, who looked unfazed.

"And as much as Mr. Abora claims to be independent, he was in Mr. Globe's pocket, so how much can we trust him?" Wineke said.

Mr. Abora shifted uncomfortably in his chair.

"I promise to be wholly independent. I plan to stand up to Mr. Globe in every way possible, including demanding that the docks go back to how they used to be. Fewer big ships, more fisherfolk."

There was a smattering of agreement and head nods from the crowd. Lillie felt a rush of pride, having suggested that line based on her conversations with the fisherfolk.

But Jeremias Scarp raised his hand. "And what's

to become of us big ship people, when Mr. Globe gives away *our* slips to the fisherfolk, eh? If you tell him he's gotta give something up, I guarantee you he won't be letting go of one of his."

Lillie bit her lip; she hadn't thought of that repercussion.

Based on Wineke's blush, neither had she. "Well, erm, I'll make sure that… Of course, he honors every agreement, and you know, whether or not he actually owns the wharf is up for debate—"

"I'll handle this, Wanda," Kathryn said, pushing her way through to the front. "So I know there's been *some* conversation about this, but I took the liberty of chatting with Samson at the library—"

"Sexton," Lillie muttered under her breath.

"And he made it quite clear to me in black and white that Mr. Globe *is* the owner of the wharf, from beginning to end, including your little fisherfolk…whatever." She waved her hand toward Orxan and Jan. "So that is to say that Mr. Globe has the final say in terms of who goes where." Kathryn surveyed the group as she grinned victoriously. "Everybody good? Mmkay. Wanda, go on—"

"Wineke," Lillie said, louder.

"Something to add, Lils?" Kathryn asked, putting her hand on her hip.

"I would appreciate it if you'd call people by their real names," Lillie said, her cheeks growing red.

"My name is Lil-*lie*, not Lils. This is Wineke Sloos, not Wanda. The McTavishes—who've been here longer than most people—are good stewards of the dock and care about being fair to the fisherfolk. And you, Kathryn, are quite rude."

Kathryn's smile widened. "Well, there's that fire Julian was telling me about."

Lillie's eyes darkened, but Wineke spoke before she could do something she'd regret. "I'd like to finish my speech if you're done interrupting."

"Well, it's clear you've said enough, eh?" Kathryn gestured to Jeremias. "But if you want to keep digging that grave, by all means, go ahead."

~

Wineke did finish her speech with no more interruptions, though Lillie barely listened to it. Her hands shook from anger, and her leg kept twitching. Next to her, Nikola and Ursil were still too hyped up by the love cake to have heard anything, and Hipolita was frowning as she watched the apothecary. From what else Lillie could see, there wasn't much interest in Wineke's campaign, especially after Kathryn had so clearly dismissed her main platform for the fisherfolk.

When it was over, Wineke plodded over to Greeley, who gave her a hug. Lillie offered her a thumbs-up, but Wineke shook her head and slipped out the back with her partner.

"Poor girl," Hipolita said next to Lillie. "You know, she's got some good ideas, but she hasn't a clue how things really work around here."

"You don't think she could accomplish what she said?" Lillie asked.

"Mr. Globe is smarter than any of us." Hipolita sighed. "And he's not one to give up power easily. If Wineke tried to take one of the dock slips, I think he'd do exactly as Jeremias said and give up his slip or May Janik's instead of one of his own."

Lillie could see that. But she could also see a scenario where Kathryn outright had lied about talking to Sexton (she hadn't used his right name, so, really, she could've been talking about anyone) to sway people away from Wineke's campaign.

Mr. Abora was next to speak. He walked to the front of the room without any notecards and smiled with more confidence than he usually had. "Good evening, friends," he began. "I want to thank you for allowing us to talk with you today. I know the Fisherfolk Council has lots to consider these days, and your support of any of these mayoral candidates would mean the world to all three of us."

"Good start," Rey muttered, having climbed up on Lillie's shoulder. "Let's see how he does."

"I know that many of you have come to me for your various issues over the years." He nodded to people in the room. "Jarvis, when there was a roof leak and you couldn't get in to see Mr. Globe. Hipolita, when you were in desperate need of help with a tax issue two years ago. Jarod, when your grandfather was having trouble with a fenceline dispute with his neighbor."

Lillie waited for him to point her out, but he didn't. Perhaps for the best, because he might *also* have to mention the blackmail.

"I'm not a perfect person, but I do feel I've done my best to serve the people of this town," he continued. "Politics and governing aren't pretty businesses. You can't make everyone happy, so you have to choose the most right thing for everyone." He straightened. "I know many of you are concerned about my connection with Mr. Globe. I think it's quite clear that by hiring Ms. Harkness to help Mr. Cast run against me, I have lost his favor. But that doesn't mean I'm powerless against him." He puffed out his chest. "It's precisely because I have worked very closely with him that I'm the best equipped to deal with him. You see, I know many of Mr. Globe's secrets. I know the deals he made to keep people happy, and I'm not afraid to use those to benefit the people of this town when it suits."

Jeremias raised his hand. "Can you do anything about the number of slips he owns?"

"Unfortunately, Ms. Harkness is right that Mr. Globe outright purchased the wharf in its entirety,"

Mr. Abora said. "But I've petitioned the king for a special allotment of magic. My vision for Silverkeep is to grow a secondary wharf, constructed by magic, that is wholly owned by the town. More for the merchants who wish to grow their presence in Silverkeep." He nodded to Jeremias. "But also more spots for any fisherfolk who wants one."

*That* seemed to be a great idea to the fisherfolk, who once again began murmuring and talking amongst themselves, this time with agreeing nods.

"*Assuming* the king answers that petition." Kathryn's voice cut through the din. "Do you know how busy that man is right now? What makes you believe you're going to be heard? Sounds like an empty promise to me."

Lillie turned to the front, wishing—praying—Mr. Abora had a response to that. But much like Wineke, he seemed caught completely off guard. "That is, I mean… The petition was sent… And he's been quite generous… And—"

"As I thought." Kathryn sauntered to the front of the room again. "Listen. He's a politician. He can say whatever he wants to make you vote for him, right? I'm sure he has, in the past. Probably has a few underhanded ways of making people do things, too, right?"

Lillie blinked. Did Kathryn know about the blackmail letters?

"I do what I do for—"

"For Mr. Globe, to make him happy, I get it. Trust me." She chuckled, patting him on the shoulder. "But if you're gonna go toe-to-toe with a man like Audo, you're going to have to have more backbone. And unfortunately, I don't see it." She smirked at Lillie. "Lils? Anything to add?"

"Careful, Lillie, she's baiting you," Rey warned.

Mr. Abora's eyes were wide behind Kathryn, as if he thought she'd told Kathryn about the blackmail letters. But, unless Kathryn had the ability to read minds, that was impossible.

"I think Mr. Abora has done a satisfactory job," Lillie said, after a moment.

"Well, he'd do better than Wanda, that's for sure," Kathryn said with another snort. "But to be honest, folks, I think we've heard enough. You know that Wanda and Carl here are going to muck things up. Who wants that? Vote for Clancy Cast, right?" She smirked. "Because *unlike* Carl, Mr. Globe actually has good contacts in King's Capital, and could actually make that wharf reality dream come true."

"How would that be any better than him owning what's already there?" Keegan asked.

"Because it's more space," Kathryn said. "Isn't that what you're all clamoring for?"

There was a begrudging agreement amongst the

crowd. Lillie looked around the room, searching for anyone who was still against Clancy, but she didn't see it. Dread sank into the pit of her stomach. Had Kathryn really won the Fisherfolk Council vote?

"Well, I think that's that."

She put her hand on her hip with a satisfied smile.

# Chapter Sixteen

"She's a loathsome creature," Rey said as they walked back to the bakery in the dark. "I mean, for her to cut everyone off like that. To be so brazen about everything. And Clancy didn't even say a word! Just let her talk. Outrageous."

"Do you think it worked?" Lillie asked.

"It's really a question of trust, isn't it?" Rey said thoughtfully. "Mr. Abora—yes, he knows how to work a system. But whether or not anyone in King's Capital has seen his request for a grant…"

"You know, it's funny. Mr. Globe has lots of friends in King's Capital," Lillie said. "I bet he could've expedited Mr. Abora's request if he had a mind to. But he won't do that because if that request is granted, he'd lose out on money."

"Or demand the fisherfolk pay him for his trouble."

Lillie hated this. Hated that Mr. Globe was so focused on making money that he couldn't even let the good people of this town have a break.

"Who're you voting for?" Rey asked.

"Wineke, if she stays in. But that was pretty defeating," Lillie said. "I know she was counting on the fisherfolk to counterbalance the nonmagicals on the other side of town. She can't win with the magicals alone."

"Agreed." Rey shook his head. "So...Mr. Abora?"

"I suppose." Lillie had been a little impressed with his thinking about using magic to grow the wharf. "He's done an okay job. Better to have him than Mr. Globe's stooge."

They reached the bakery, and Lillie was fumbling with her keys when the apothecary door opened, and Greeley popped his head out.

"How's Wineke?" Lillie asked.

"Devastated. She's going to pull out of the mayoral race." He shook his head. "I tried to convince her otherwise, but she's pretty sure."

"I'm glad you were there," Lillie said. "I know it

meant a lot to her to have your support."

"Thank Fawn. She was yelling at me to get out of there for at least half an hour, but…" He looked around, a smile teasing the corners of his mouth. "But I had to finish the experiment. Because I think we found the poison. The pernicula flower."

Dread and relief swam in her mind. They had an answer, at least.

"It doesn't affect pobyds, as Fawn thought," Greeley said. "It can cause illness in nonmagical people, as we saw, but its main purpose is to trigger magic. But…" He chewed his lip. "Here's the thing. It needs magic at first to sort of…wake up, if that makes sense."

"What does that mean?" Rey asked.

"It means you triggered the poison when you used pobyd magic to make them more delicious," Greeley said.

"But the lemon cookies didn't have magic in them," Lillie said with a frown. "I intentionally remove it for…" She cleared her throat. "Reasons."

"Did you use magic at any point during the creation?"

"Well, I suppose so, to make the butter—"

"Then the poison would've been activated," Greeley said.

Lillie ran a hand over her face. This was starting to feel *really* personal.

"We tested the rest of the cupcakes once we had the poison identified," Greeley continued. "We found traces of it in both the buttercream *and* the crumb."

"Really?"

"I made sure to test both separately just to make sure," Greeley said, a little excitedly. I don't think that there was cross-contamination, either."

"So it's an ingredient in both," Lillie said, more to herself. "Either milk, sugar, chocolate, or…well, I doubt it would be the vanilla bean." Nor the chocolate, because Lillie had clearly used magic on the same batch of chocolate in Julian's bakery when she'd made the Kovens' cake. "The bigger question now is when did they add the poison? Did they break into my shop to do it, or did it come poisoned from the supplier?"

"You think your suppliers would do something like that?" Rey frowned.

"If they were paid enough money, maybe," Lillie said. "And if the goal was to run me out of business, too—which is starting to look like the case. I mean, you saw Kathryn tonight." She bristled as the memory came to the forefront. "How very *convenient* that she had Julian's baked goods ready to go. She knows the bulk of my customers come from the wharf—and I heard more than a few folks say they'd have to try Julian's shop now that he's baking better."

"I hate her triple now," Rey said.

"She seems to have the measure of everyone in town," Greeley said heavily. "I wish I could've done something to stop her from derailing Wineke's campaign."

"I fear Jeremias did that for her," Rey said.

"Well, if you'd like, I can get started on testing your ingredients to find the source of the poison," Greeley said, after a moment.

"Absolutely not," Lillie said with a meaningful look. "You need to get upstairs and support your partner. I'll bring the stuff over tomorrow. We're not going to be in trouble if we wait a night to test, but Wineke will remember that you weren't there for her."

Greeley nodded, his cheeks flushing. "Erm. Right. What should I...say to her?"

"To Wineke?" Lillie smiled. Greeley was incredibly brilliant, but communication wasn't his strong suit. "Just listen. Hold her hand. Tell her that it's terrible. Don't try to reason with her or say that Kathryn made *any* good points. Be on her side. And let her talk."

"I can handle that," Greeley said, seemingly jotting down mental notes as if this were another one of his experiments.

"Greeley." Lillie laughed. "Just be there for her."

She nodded toward the front door. "Now go."

~

After the apothecary scampered upstairs, Lillie and Rey stood in the front room of the bakery to make sense of what they'd learned.

"Well, now we've really got something going, don't we?" Rey said, rubbing his hands together.

Lillie considered the sugar, pinching it between her fingers and wishing she could tell what was wrong with it—if anything. "I'd like to believe someone broke into the bakery, Rey. But I'm pretty good at locking the doors when I'm not here. Unless someone came in through your mousehole—"

"Decidedly not," Rey said with a loud harrumph.

"Then I fear it might be one of my suppliers. I sincerely hope not, of course, but after my talk with the Casts, I can't be too sure. And Kathryn's made no attempt to hide that she's trying to ruin my business." Among other things.

"She can talk, but the people of Silverkeep know you, Lillie," Rey said. "Many of them owe you for saving their bacon, too."

"And others hate me for taking it," Lillie said, thinking of Mr. Globe.

"Who do you get sugar from again?" Rey asked.

"Eduardo down at the wharf market," Lillie said. "Lovely guy. Never said a bad word against me, but

I do think it's worth it to talk with him. And..." She sighed. "Well, the milk obviously comes from Esmerelda, so I should talk with her, too."

"Esmerelda Honeygold hasn't been very friendly toward you," Rey said. "Perhaps she's trying to get you to drop her as a supplier."

"I don't think so," Lillie said. "Because she asked me to make butter for her this morning. And she told me herself the farm is struggling. That's not the time to get rid of your best customer."

"Unless maybe one of them secretly really wants to sell it?" Rey suggested. "Maybe trying to sabotage the business so the others feel there's no choice but to sell."

"But why?" Lillie leaned her elbows on the table. "If it's that bad, just close it."

"The others don't want to?" Rey suggested.

*That* was a possibility. Kristin would surely be heartbroken to lose her family home, and Lillie didn't know Esmerelda that well, but she had a feeling she was happy in her familial home.

"There's no use in speculating motives until we chat with everyone, I suppose," Lillie said. "Either way, these aren't going to be very pleasant conversations tomorrow."

~

When morning rolled around, Lillie considered what, if anything, she could possibly make to sell, but very quickly realized that it was pretty much impossible to bake anything without sugar. Instead, she brought Greeley everything she wanted tested, and he promised he'd get right on it, leaving her free to wander the market—and ask the questions she needed.

The wharf was thankfully quite busy, and Lillie gave a brief nod to Esmerelda as she passed. She wanted to save that awkward conversation for last. Eduardo was at his post, small pouches of sugar displayed on the wooden counter for all to see. His smile faltered when he spotted Lillie, and her suspicions grew.

"Good morning, Eduardo!" she said, trying to keep herself neutral.

"Ah, good morning, Ms. Dean." He recovered from his initial shock. "It's a little early for you to get your next sugar order. I'm not quite ready for you yet."

Lillie eyed him, watching for any sign of guilt. Was it simply that he didn't have the product for her, or was he covering for something else? "Well, it turns out I had to toss everything you gave me. Someone poisoned it."

His eyes widened and his mouth fell open. "Is that why I got so ill after the Fisherfolk Council meeting?"

"Erm." Lillie had completely forgotten he'd

been there. Perhaps he wasn't the poisoner. "Yes. I think someone's sabotaging me."

"Outrageous!" Eduardo jumped to his feet and puffed out his chest. "I won't stand for it. No, I won't. Who in their right mind would want to disrupt the business of a kind person such as yourself? Absolutely not, I won't—"

"I think it's Audo Globe," Lillie admitted.

He sank down onto his stool. "Well, in that case, I'm terribly sorry for your loss."

Lillie couldn't help laughing. "That bad, huh?"

"If Audo Globe wants you out of business, you're going out of business." He shook his head. "Why in the world would he want to sabotage you? And how?"

"I was going to ask you the same question," Lillie said. "We're still trying to figure out which ingredient it was, but Greeley Sloos is getting close. We've narrowed it down to the milk, chocolate, or…sugar."

He screwed up his face and pressed his hand to his heart. "I swear to you, Ms. Dean, on my beloved mother's life, that I would *never* do anything to harm you."

"Even if Mr. Globe paid you to do it?" Lillie asked. "I hear he's been telling people they can only sell to Globe Café."

"Pshaw. I'd sell to you under the table, if he

tried that." Eduardo smirked. "But no, he hasn't come to me. I deliver sugar to Globe Café, and I sell a ten-pound bag to you every third day here. You two are my best customers." He nodded toward Esmerelda's booth, which was farther up the market. "Now, I'm not sure where you get your chocolate, but I'd probably point my finger at the Honeygolds. I've heard rumors about them lately."

"What kind of rumors?" Lillie asked.

"They're in money trouble. Lots of it. They've always scraped by, but lately, it's gotten worse. Lots of folks want to buy up land—the Casts sold their farm to some high and mighty person from Sheepsburg. Esmerelda's wife's been talking about selling to them, too, but Esmerelda and Kristin are against it, as I understand."

Lillie bit her lip. She really, *really* didn't want to walk down that route, but it was looking unavoidable. "That's not great to hear. I really didn't want to believe it was someone I've done business with."

"Desperation makes for strange bedfellows," Eduardo said with a shrug. "I don't have a large bag of sugar to sell you, but I could sell you a couple smaller ones."

"I'm closed today until we figure all this out," Lillie said. "But I appreciate the offer—and the loyalty. I'm glad to have you in my corner,

Eduardo."

He bowed. "As always, m'dear."

Lillie considered returning to the apothecary instead of having an uncomfortable conversation with Esmerelda. She meandered around for half an hour, muttering to herself as she sorted out what she was going to say and how she was going to say it. If she was wrong, and the Honeygolds weren't responsible, she might destroy a relationship that had just been mended.

And if she was right… She didn't want to think about it.

Esmerelda looked happy to see her (in that she didn't scowl when Lillie approached), and Lillie braced herself for an awful conversation.

"I'm glad you're here," Esmerelda said. "I didn't stop by this morning, since, you know, you're still closed." She paused. "Right?"

"Mm." Lillie nodded with some difficulty.

"But I could really use a few pounds of butter for the crowd," Esmerelda said with a hopeful look. "If you don't mind."

"I'm happy to, except…" Lillie held her breath. "We've isolated the poison that's been making everyone sick. It's either in the sugar or…your milk." She swallowed. "No other customers have been complaining about anything, right?"

She frowned. "No, they haven't. Not at all." She

blanched as the insinuation became clear to her. "Our milk is the highest quality. We would *never* consider selling anything that wasn't… I hope you aren't spreading nasty rumors about us, Ms. Dean."

"I'm not saying anything," Lillie said, holding up her hands in defense. "But the facts are—"

"If you have a problem with our product, you can surely shop somewhere else. But I'll *thank you* to keep from disparaging our family when we're already in such dire straits."

Lillie could've stood there and tried to explain herself, but something else had popped up into her mind. It very well could've been someone else at Honeygold Farms. Someone who wanted to sell, and perhaps…someone who handled the milk and set those jugs aside especially for Lillie.

"I'm sorry I even mentioned it," Lillie said. "Would you like me to make that butter for you?"

"No. Perhaps you're poisoning it yourself and looking for someone to blame." Esmerelda lifted her chin. "Good *day*, Ms. Dean."

Unfortunately, the results from Greeley were as concerning as Esmerelda's reaction.

"The sugar is fine," he said. "So is the flour, and even the lemon rinds. I tested samples from the top, bottom, and middle of the bag, just to be sure. Everything's perfectly safe for consumption."

Lillie exhaled, pinching the bridge of her nose. She really, *really* hadn't wanted to hear that. "I see. So it's the milk. Probably."

"Or the vanilla," Greeley suggested half-heartedly. "But I think you'd have to have a lot of vanilla to cause the sort of reactions we've seen. I believe I can say with some confidence that it's the milk."

She returned to the bakery with a heart heavy with regret and annoyance. On the one hand, it was nice to have an answer. She could bake to her heart's content—and didn't have to throw out nearly ten pounds of sugar—but one of her dearest friend's products was the source of the poison. And clearly, her sister either didn't know or didn't want Lillie finding out.

Lillie replayed the times she'd purchased milk from them since Kristin broke her leg. The first time, Esmerelda had given her a crate of milk that had been tied with yellow ribbons—clearly intended for her. The second time had been much the same. Lillie had thought it nice that someone had set aside her standing order, especially since Esmerelda was decidedly *un*friendly toward her, but now…

Was it intentional?

She hoisted the crate of empty milk bottles onto her table and inspected each one for any lingering milk. Of course, before everything had happened, she'd cleaned and rinsed the bottles so they'd be ready to fill again. She was being *proactive*, as she always was, because Kristin usually took the empty bottles when she delivered the fresh set, and Lillie didn't like the thought of them sitting out all day in the sun unclean.

If she'd only known she was rinsing out evidence.

She replaced the bottles and sighed. After the conversation with Esmerelda, she really, *really* didn't want to keep poking the bear, but the facts were clear—and Lillie needed answers. But she wasn't about to make the trek alone this time.

"Hey, Rey?" Lillie called as she straightened. "Are you here?"

"At your service." Rey appeared out of the mousehole. "What's going on?"

"We need to head up to Honeygold Farms," Lillie said.

"You spoke to Greeley, then?" He shook his head. "Fawn told me they'd found the answer. It defies logic they'd do this to you, Lillie."

"It does and it doesn't," she said with a half-smile. "I hear they're thinking of selling their farm, so I want to sniff around."

"I don't think the Honeygolds are going to tell you anything, are they?"

"Mm. Probably not me, but *you* know someone who might've heard something, don't you?" Lillie asked with a smirk. "A Penelope Bigears, perhaps?"

Rey groaned. "Oh, Lillie, she's *awful.* Don't make me speak with her. Bad enough when she comes down to the Silverkeep Inn."

"You know as well as I do that she probably

hears more than the Honeygolds want her to," Lillie said. "And if there's something afoot, she'd know it."

"*Fine.*"

~

They set off at once, with a brief stop at the magical texts and tomes shop to barter books. Esmerelda had said Kristin had read every book in the house, and if Lillie was coming to bear bad news, she didn't want to come empty-handed. With two books on the basics of growing magical flora in her arms (because those were the only things she could purchase for a single silver), she headed up the hill toward the square with Rey perched on her shoulder.

"What, exactly, am I talking to Penelope about?" he asked.

"Well, I've got a few theories on how this might've happened," Lillie said, lowering her voice as they reached the square. "The first is that Charla wants to sell the farm. The sisters are resisting. So she's done something to the milk so I'll stop buying from them. They lose their best customer, they have no choice but to sell."

"Solid reasoning," Rey said. "What's the second theory?"

"That Mr. Globe—or someone working on his behalf—offered Esmerelda a lot of money to poison my milk, specifically, so I would go out of business," Lillie said.

"Oh, that would be awful," Rey said with a sigh.

Lillie nodded. "I have a horrid feeling there was a stipulation in there that they wouldn't get any money if my business remains open, which means this won't stop until one of us gives." She chewed her lip. "I'm devastated for Kristin. She never would've allowed this to happen if she hadn't broken her leg."

"She'll be happy to see you, anyway," Rey said. "Even if you are about to suggest her family is doing horrible things in the name of gold."

As they walked through the square, Lillie's gaze drifted toward Globe Café, and a rush of anger flooded her cheeks. Not necessarily at Julian, of course, though he was much farther down on her list of people she liked than he used to be. But Kathryn, who Lillie could see handling all this evildoing for Mr. Globe. Demanding that "Elizabeth" (Esmerelda) and "Carrie" (Charla) pour a bit of this poison into the milk they'd set aside for Lillie, and they'd get all kinds of gold in return.

"Why are you so red?" Rey asked. "Are you getting overheated?"

"No, just thinking," Lillie said, forcing herself to look ahead instead of at Julian's business. "The sooner this stupid election is finished, the better."

That was assuming, of course, that Mr. Globe didn't find another job for Kathryn in Silverkeep. Lillie could barely stand the thought.

The walk to the Honeygolds' farm did wonders to soften Lillie's mood, and by the time she knocked on the front door, she was holding only a *small* grudge for Kathryn Harkness instead of a full-blown vendetta.

"Okay, you go find Penelope," she told Rey as she put him down. "I'll be in the living room with Kristin."

"Ugh. Do I really have to?" Rey asked, tugging on his small vest. "She's such a pain."

"Rey."

"Fine. Fine." He waved her off as he walked toward the edge of the porch. "The things I do for you, Lillie Dean. I expect an extra-chocolatey chocolate chip cookie for payment."

"Find me what I need to know, and you'll get two," Lillie said, and meant it.

He disappeared off the porch as the door opened. Kristin, who looked tired and haggard, brightened immediately when she spotted Lillie. "Oh! What a surprise! Come in, come in!"

It was still very clear that Kristin was all but living in the front room, and Lillie resisted the urge to tidy up, seeing as Charla had given her a lecture before for the generous thought. Kristin hobbled over to the couch and settled in, moving blankets around so it didn't look like a bed.

"Here. Two new books for you," Lillie said, placing them on the stack of other books. "Esmerelda said you'd read everything else."

"Twice," Kristin said with a sigh. "Gosh, I'm so happy to see you. I've been bored out of my mind. The most excitement I've had is that our cows got into the wrong field again because Charla left the gate open. You shoulda seen me shooing them back where they needed to go with my crutches. It was a *mess*." She laughed. "Essi said you were making her butter, but that you were closed for some reason. Is your oven okay? Don't tell me it broke again."

"No, of course not." Lillie tried not to read too much into the fact that Esmerelda hadn't told Kristin Lillie's pastries had been poisoned. "You haven't heard about the Fisherfolk Council or any of that?"

"I know the election is happening, but otherwise..." Kristin frowned. "What's going on?"

Lillie told her everything, save the part where she suspected the poisoning was coming from her own product. Kristin's brows rose higher at each twist, including when it turned out that Lillie's cupcakes had caused a great deal of magical mischief at Mr. Abora's campaign rally.

"That's terrible, Lillie. Who do you think is

behind it?"

Lillie swallowed. "Well, Greeley tested one of the leftover cupcakes, and there was a pobyd-resistant poison in both parts of the cupcake. So we've narrowed the issue to either the sugar, the chocolate, or—"

"The milk." Kristin sat back. "Don't tell me that's what you think it is. Lillie, I swear to you, we'd never do anything like that. You're our best customer. You're my friend."

"I know," Lillie said with a tight smile. "And I want to get to the bottom of what happened. From what Greeley said, this poison is only reactive after someone adds magic to it. It would only make people sick after it came from my kitchen, after I used pobyd magic on it." She braced herself. "The poison was most likely added to the milk before I got it."

"Or maybe someone broke into the bakery and added it," Kristin said. "Did you think about that?"

"It's possible," Lillie admitted. "But the first day—the Fisherfolk Council—I'd gotten the milk from your sister and used it without leaving it alone. And that milk had been specifically set aside for me."

Kristin swallowed. "That's because I told her to. I didn't want her to sell out of what we'd agreed to—especially because she said she wasn't going to deliver to you. It took a lot of convincing to even get her to set anything aside for you." She stared out the window. "This doesn't make any sense, Lillie."

"I know it's hard to believe, but—"

"No, I mean... My sister and Charla aren't stupid, by any means, but they're not exactly *learned* in things like poisons. I don't know what would be triggered by pobyd magic, and I read far more than they do."

"I fear someone might've given it to them."

Kristin's mouth fell open. "Who?"

"Someone with a lot of money, who might've taken advantage of a farm falling on tough times," Lillie said quietly. "You guys haven't...come into any new money, have you?"

Kristin bit her lip, staring at the door. "Nobody's told me anything, but...I can't believe they'd do something like that, Lillie. I know, it seems obvious, and they haven't been the nicest to you, but they're not mean people, you know? They're not going to be swayed by money or..." She exhaled. "At least, I hope they wouldn't."

"What's going on with that, anyway? I heard Charla wants to sell the farm?"

Kristin shrugged and sank back into the floral print of the couch. "She's never really recovered from when the queen's folks took her brother and our parents. She says this farm is full of ghosts, and she's ready to leave them behind." She exhaled. "But

I'm not. This is our family's home. We've managed to survive all this time. We're not going to give up when things get tough."

Lillie nodded. "I'm not trying to cause any problems. Goodness knows, with your leg, you guys have plenty. But I need to figure out how this happened, and whether or not—"

"What in the world are *you* doing here?" Charla stood in the doorway to the backyard, her overalls covered in mud and muck, and her cheeks flushed. "I thought we explicitly told you to stay off our property."

"Char, be nice," Kristin said, shifting with some difficulty. "Lillie's here to—"

"I don't care why she's here. She's not allowed. And if she doesn't leave right this second—"

"I'm trying to figure out if the milk you sold me poisoned everyone at the Fisherfolk Council, among others," Lillie said pointedly.

Charla's mouth fell open. "We didn't *sell you poisoned milk*."

"Well, you sold it to me. It was poisoned." Lillie quirked a brow.

"If you sold subpar baked goods, that's none of our concern," Charla said with a glower. "I think it's time you find another source for your milk."

"Absolutely not," Kristin said, hobbling to her feet. "Lillie's our best customer. We can't possibly survive without her."

"Then we'll fold," Charla said. "Sell the farm. It happens all the time."

Lillie's brow furrowed. "I hear you're the only one who feels that way, Charla."

"This is a *family* discussion," Charla said hotly. "You, pobyd, are not family. So please leave before I ask the sheriff to have you removed."

Lillie tried to imagine Juno coming out to remove her and snorted. "I'm going. But please understand that I'm only trying to help—"

"You're trying to save your business," Charla said. "I was in town recently. Everyone's talking about how you poisoned the fisherfolk, among others. So it's no surprise you're here, trying to pin the blame on us."

"The apothecary found the poison, not me," Lillie said.

"Another magical? How *convenient*."

Lillie pursed her lips and rose stiffly. "Well. I can see I'm wasting my time here. Kristin, I do hope your leg heals quickly. Once you're back on your feet, we can talk about resuming our business arrangement. In the meantime, I'll find a different supplier until I know what's going on."

"Lillie, please don't go," Kristin said.

"Enjoy those books," Lillie said with a kind smile. "I'm sorry they're so drab, but it's the best I could do under the circumstances. At the moment, I'm quite strapped for coins myself, what with someone out to destroy my business." She turned to Charla. "Good day to you, Ms. Honeygold."

~

Luckily, Rey was waiting on the front porch when Lillie exited, and she scooped him up and placed him on her shoulder.

"Tell me you heard something," Lillie muttered under her breath. "Anything. Right now, all I have is a hunch—and two people acting like I'm evil incarnate."

"Penelope is such a bear to speak with," Rey said with a sigh. "But she did confirm there are money troubles—most of it stemming from the Casts selling their farm."

"Really?" Lillie shook her head. "Why?"

"Being neighbors, there was a lot of stuff they got together, like grass seed and tools and things like that. Quantity discount, you know. So now that the Casts are gone, the Honeygolds are having to pay full price for it."

"What are the new neighbors growing?"

"Penelope didn't know. They've been ripping up the fields for something or another. Penelope heard a rumor they're going to build new homes for some magical folks who've come out of hiding, but that's at least the fifth story she's heard."

Lillie glanced behind her at the disappearing farmhouse. "I see."

"Esmerelda keeps talking about buying some tanddaes again, but Charla refuses. Says they won't get bitten twice."

"I can understand the sentiment," Lillie said. "Mr. Globe has a similar feeling."

"About what?" Rey frowned. "Who's got magic in his family, other than his wife? But she's long gone."

"Just...in general," Lillie said evasively. She'd really have to work on what she spilled to Rey—Julian's sister Odetta was a budding mage, but Mr. Globe was keeping that completely under wraps for some reason. That Rey and the Small Folk Network didn't know was a testament to his dedication to keeping it a secret.

That, or he paid anyone living in his house to keep their tiny mouths shut.

"There's more," Rey said. "Penelope said Esmerelda was talking about money coming in soon. That she'd made some kind of arrangement—Penelope didn't know specifics."

Lillie stopped. "What?"

"Yeah, she didn't have any details. Just that Esmerelda wasn't ready to sell the farm yet," Rey said. "It wasn't a done deal, though."

"Nothing with Mr. Globe ever is," Lillie

muttered, looking back at the farmhouse in the distance.

"Is it time to talk with Juno?" Rey asked. "We've got some evidence. We've got the source of the poison. Maybe she can investigate. Get the Honeygolds to confess to it."

"I'm sure she'd tell me I messed up the butter all by myself," Lillie said. "Remember, she's on Mr. Globe's payroll, too. No, I think it's time we talk directly with the source of all this trouble."

"You just left the Honeygolds...?"

"Not them. Kathryn Harkness."

Rey scratched his whiskers. "Do we really know she's responsible, though?"

"We have a lot of evidence," Lillie said. "She's new. She works for Mr. Globe. She's not above lying to people or bribing them to get what she wants."

"Yes, but—"

"And she clearly wants me out of town," Lillie finished, though she was at least smart enough not to give a reason why. "It's time I confronted her—really confronted her. And demand the truth."

"If you say so..."

Lillie glared at him. "Are you on my side or not?"

"Always." He laughed nervously. "Lead the way."

Lillie and Rey arrived at the Silverkeep town square, which was starting to fill up in advance of the mayoral election this evening. Officially, the town hall would open for the final speeches and voting around five this evening, but some of the sailors and merchants were already milling about in the square—and at Globe Café, which was busier than Lillie had expected at this time of day. She inspected her outfit nervously, but there was nothing to be done about it. She was going in as she was, even though Kathryn would look better. Lillie needed to have this confrontation.

"Well?" Rey said, bouncing on her shoulder. "Are we ready to contend with this foe? Get the truth? Find out what she knows and get her to come out with it?"

"That's the plan," Lillie said.

"And what if she tells you she had nothing to do with it?" Rey prompted.

"If the Honeygolds have come into money, there's probably only one source. Maybe I'll offer to pay her double what Mr. Globe is."

"You can't afford that."

"Well!" Lillie bristled. "Whatever. I'll play it by ear. But I'm tired of her smug little smile and the way she wears those expensive clothes and her perfect hair and..." She stopped, realizing she might be revealing too much. "She deserves to be put in her place."

"Hear, hear," Rey said. "Let's go!"

Lillie marched over to the café with all the confidence she didn't exactly feel. The smell of fresh coffee hit her nose right away, reminding her acutely of the moment when coffee-flavored lips had touched hers. She willed the memory and the blush to go away. Julian had very clearly not wanted to do that. And she wasn't about to dwell on him anymore—not when she had to get answers.

But neither Julian nor Kathryn were in the front room of the café, which was buzzing with people.

The pastries on the table looked passable, if not downright skilled in some areas. There were unfamiliar faces (probably staying at the inn next door), along with the usual suspects. Zena Plotter was seated at a table nearby, reading a book, and scoffed when she spotted Lillie.

"Are you lost?"

"No," Lillie said. "I'm looking for Kathryn."

"Thankfully, she's gone for the moment," Zena said, idly turning the page of her book. "She's absolutely dreadful to listen to."

"So you haven't sold her anything lately?" Lillie asked. Not that she thought Zena would be responsible, but it couldn't hurt to ask. "Perhaps a pernicula flower?"

"W-what in the world is that?" Zena said before she could stop herself. "I mean, of course I've heard of that. Very common flower. Why would I be selling it to Kathryn?"

Lillie did her best to hide a smile. "Well, because it's the reason everyone's been so sick after eating my pastries."

"I...see..." She seemed to reconsider her confidence. "When I said I've heard of it, I meant that I'm familiar with the concept. I haven't actually *seen* it, and goodness knows I don't have any in stock in my store—"

"I'm sure you don't," Lillie said with a kind

smile.

"But you think I've been poisoning your customers?" She laughed. "You are but a speck on my long list of enemies. I barely give you or that perfidious little mouse who nearly ruined my shop a second thought."

Lillie sincerely doubted that. "Actually, I was wondering where someone might get some." *Especially since you clearly had no idea what it was.*

"Why don't you ask your apothecary friends?" Zena said pointedly. "I'm not in the habit of giving out information for free, you know."

"Of course not," Lillie said with a nod. "Thank you for—"

But she stopped short. Julian had emerged from the back room wearing an apron and short-sleeved white shirt, a casual and joyful smile on his face.

Gosh. He was *handsome.*

He picked up a shiny silver carafe, pouring coffee into three waiting cups with an infectious smile. A single strand of dark brown hair had curled onto his forehead, and his apron was smeared with flour and chocolate. He moved with a confidence that said he was exactly where he was meant to be, and it made Lillie happy.

"*That was a mistake.*"

Reality tumbled into place, and Lillie's heart pounded. He wasn't interested in her, clearly, and

Lillie would do well to remember that.

Then, as if he'd heard her thoughts, his eyes met hers. They widened—Shock? Fear? Lillie couldn't tell—and he licked his lips, as if ready to call out, to announce to the world that he no longer felt the same about her.

"We should leave," Lillie muttered to Rey.

But as she spun toward the door, the very person she'd been meaning to talk with came sauntering through. Kathryn, too, looked comfortable in the bakery, with her perfectly curled hair fanning out around her face, a bag hanging from her arm, and an obnoxious bit of gum that popped as she spoke.

"Well, isn't this a surprise?" she crowed, loud enough that everyone in the café heard. "Dropping off a bit of poison to your competition, Lils?"

"Asking questions about where it might've come from, actually," Rey replied coolly from Lillie's shoulder. "The local apothecaries were able to find out what it was. The pernicula flower. Activated by magic, and pobyd-resistant. Seems like someone did it intentionally to ruin Lillie's business."

"Did they?" Kathryn's brows went up. "Well, don't make enemies, and you might not have to worry about someone sabotaging you."

"Now see here," Rey began, stomping his foot on Lillie's shoulder. "Lillie's done nothing except try to do the right thing for everyone in this town—"

"That's not what I hear," Kathryn said with a smirk.

Lillie's blood ran cold. If she worked for Mr. Globe, would he have told her about Lillie's past in Lower Pigsend? Was that why Julian had suddenly changed his mind about her?

"Right or wrong," Lillie managed, after a moment, "that doesn't give you an excuse to poison people."

"I think the only one poisoning people is you," Kathryn said. "You know that pernicula is part of a family of herbs that only activate when magic is applied, right? If Julian baked those same pastries, nobody would've ever known. It's really your fault, if you think about it."

"Now, Kathryn," Julian's low voice echoed behind Lillie, "that's not fair."

Lillie refused to turn around, not even when the hair on her neck rose at his proximity.

"I'm stating facts, Jules," Kathryn said, shrugging.

*Jules?* Lillie's eyes filled with spots as anger surged in her chest. She needed to leave this place before she did something she regretted.

"I don't know how much Mr. Globe is paying you—" Lillie said through clenched teeth.

"Clearly, not enough."

"—but taking advantage of poor farmers on the

brink of disaster isn't fair to anyone," Lillie said. "And I don't know how much you've paid the Honeygolds, but—"

"Who're they?" Kathryn asked. "I mean, I know there are a *lot* of podunk people in this town, but I don't think I've met them."

Lillie snorted. "I'm sure. You probably stopped in after you convinced Clancy Cast to sell his farm. Told them if they poisoned my milk, they'd get a nice payday, hm?"

"I didn't convince him of anything," Kathryn said. "You sure do have a lot of bad information, Lils."

"My. Name. Is. Lil-*lie*," Lillie snarled, blood pumping in her ears. "I'm not your friend, and I'm certainly not amicable enough with you that I'm allowing a nickname." She chanced a look at Julian, who seemed helpless as he stared between the two of them. "I know you made a deal with Esmerelda Honeygold. Probably something like if my business folded, they'd get a payment of some kind. Mr. Globe likes to make deals like that, contingent on getting what he wants." Lillie pointed at Kathryn. "But know this, I'm *not* going to take this abuse lying down. If I have to bring the entirety of King's Capital down on you, I will. I've worked too hard on this bakery to give it up without a fight."

And with that, Lillie stormed out of Globe Café.

~

"Lils, wait!"

Lillie was halfway back to her bakery when Julian's voice stopped her in her tracks. He ran over to her, panting and out of breath.

"What do you want?" Lillie snapped, unable to keep the tears out of her voice. "Here to tell me that your girlfriend couldn't possibly have poisoned my goods because she's perfect in every way? That—"

"Girlfrie...what?" He straightened, shaking his head. "Lils, what are you talking about?"

"Lil-*lie*," she said. "And you two have clearly been talking, haven't you? Reliving old times, right? Having a big ol' laugh about Lillie Dean—"

He took her hand, stopping her short. "Lillie, she asked me about you. I gave her one-word answers." He lifted her chin with a finger. "Whatever she learned about you, it wasn't from me."

"Get your hands off her, you cad!" Rey cried from Lillie's shoulder.

Julian stepped back as if Lillie were on fire, but for once, Lillie wasn't upset that Rey was interrupting a moment between them. "She called me Lils. Where'd she get that from?"

"I mean." He chuckled. "That's a pretty obvious shortening of your name. She's big on nicknames—whether people like them or not."

Lillie scowled at him. "Julian, this is serious. She's poisoned nearly the entire population down at the wharf. Then Mr. Abora's campaign rally, too. My business has been closed for days. I can't afford this."

Julian blinked, confused. "Wait, you think *Kathryn's* behind it? What's all that about the Honeygolds?"

"They're about to lose their farm," Lillie said.

"That's funny, considering Kristin Honeygold told me she'd never sell to me," Julian muttered.

Lillie ignored that. "Rey heard that they've got something 'in the works' to earn some quick gold. Now suddenly I'm sold poisoned milk? Seems like someone's paying them off to ruin me."

Julian's eyes filled with concern. "Lils—"

"No." She couldn't bear to see him act concerned, especially after he'd called their kiss a mistake. "No, I don't need your pity."

"Then what do you need from me?"

Her heart skipped. She needed so many things from him—but with effort, she wrenched her thoughts back to the most pressing issue. "I need evidence that she struck a deal with the Honeygolds. I need the poison itself—wherever she might've gotten it from. Clearly not Greeley, and clearly not Zena, because Zena'd never heard of it before." Lillie swallowed. "And I need help convincing Juno to press charges."

"I'm willing to do all of that and more," Julian said, taking a hesitant step toward her. "Except I don't think Kathryn did it. That's not her style."

"Oh." Lillie took a step back. "I've heard all about how much you know of her *style.* You two have a history. You never mentioned that to me."

He flinched. "You heard about that?"

"She was very upfront about it," Lillie said.

"We dated years ago." Julian inched closer, but his gaze went to Rey on her shoulder. "You shouldn't worry about that."

Lillie could've screamed. "Just because you have a history doesn't mean she's not poisoning people, Julian."

"If she's going to destroy you, she'll do it to your face, not underhanded like spiking a bowl of punch —or a batch of pastries." He chuckled darkly. "Trust me. I know more than most."

"Well, she and Jarvis were the only ones still standing at the Fisherfolk Council," Rey pointed out.

"Another reason she probably isn't behind it. She'd make sure to cover her tracks better than leaving herself the only suspect."

Lillie didn't like how complimentary he was being. "Well, her face is... Her hair is... I mean—"

"Lillie Dean." Julian grinned. "Are you jealous?"

Her entire body flushed, and she shook her head. "No, I just—" She shook her head. "Your father forbade the new owners of Clancy Cast's farm from selling me milk. Now my primary milk supplier is selling me poisoned milk—and there's now a mysterious extra payment coming to them for something. You want to tell me that's not intentional?"

"Well, first of all, he's not in charge of the Casts' farm anymore," Julian said. "So he can't forbid anyone from doing anything. But if you heard that they won't sell you any milk, it's because they're not selling milk at all. They're converting the farm to something else." He exhaled. "Which is actually a problem for me, because now I have to find another dairy farmer. I'd go to the Honeygolds, but Kristin told me she'd rather die than sell me a single jug."

"That seems short-sighted of her," Lillie managed, not wanting to think about either of them at the moment.

"We need to talk about the other night," Julian said quietly, glancing at Rey. "When you get a minute."

"No, we don't," Lillie said, snapping back to reality. "I heard you loud and clear. It was a mistake."

"That's not…" He sighed. "Let me explain myself. Please."

"You said everything you needed to." Lillie lifted her chin to meet his gaze. "And if you're not going to help me, I'll keep looking for the truth on my own. Good day to you, Mr. Globe."

This time, she didn't turn around when he called her name.

Typically, Lillie felt much better walking through the front door of her bakery, but today, all it did was serve as a reminder that she'd been betrayed by the ones she loved most in this town. First by Julian, who, judging by how eager he was to defend her, was very happy with Kathryn by his side. Then by Kristin, who probably had nothing to do with Lillie's milk getting poisoned. But it still hurt.

Rey was still hopping mad about Julian and his *forwardness,* as Rey put it. "He takes too many liberties. Just like his father, you know. Thinks he owns everything in this town." He finally stopped ranting long enough to take the measure of Lillie. "Are you all right?"

"Fine." Lillie wasn't, but she felt the need to put on a brave face. "I'm going to open the bakery. Make what I can without butter."

"Which is...?"

"Not much," Lillie admitted. "But I refuse to let them win."

Macarons were the answer, which required almond meal, egg whites, sugar—and for the filling, Lillie would use a fruit jam. Lillie felt a certain kind of joy pulverizing the almonds (she did them by hand, to get the rest of her frustrations out) and firing up the oven. She didn't even feel a twinge of sadness that the last time she'd made macarons was with Julian, when her oven had been out and someone had requested them specifically. No, she was floating on air as she mixed the egg whites until they were frothy then added dehydrated strawberry powder to them, and hummed as she piped the macarons onto baking sheets.

"Lillie?" Wineke called from the front room. "Are you...open?"

Lillie poked her head out of the kitchen. "Wineke! Come in. Yes, I'm...well, I'm not open, but I'm baking. Macarons."

"Good for you," Wineke said with a sigh as she

leaned on the counter. "At least someone's having a good day."

"Greeley told me," Lillie said. "How're you holding up?"

"I mean…" She shrugged. "Don't feel like I can show my face anywhere in town anymore. Especially not at the wharf."

"I feel the same way," Lillie said. "I shouldn't have gone with you last night. I fear it made everything worse."

"No, I'm so glad you were there," Wineke said. "And Greeley, too, though he said he was late because he'd figured out what the poison was." She chuckled, shaking her head. "You'da thought he'd discovered the cure for dragon's breath the way he was carrying on."

"I hope he was being supportive of you," Lillie said with a scowl. "I lectured him—"

"Trust me, there were only so many ways I could tell him how upset I was without sounding repetitive," she said. "Besides that, when Greeley's happy, I'm happy. And he was *so* pleased with himself that he solved that puzzle for you."

"If only he could tell me how it got into the milk, then we'd really be in business," Lillie said with a sigh.

"Well, he went down to the wharf to get a jug from Honeygold Farms," Wineke said. "By his logic, if there's something in the milk he got, they didn't poison yours intentionally. But if there's nothing..." She lifted a shoulder. "Besides that, if he brings back a jug and it's *not* poisoned, you can use it to make me something to raise my spirits."

Lillie grinned. "I like that thinking. I figured macarons were the safest thing to make because they require no butter, but there's not much else on that list." She gestured toward the small discs drying out in the back. "The bigger problem is I don't know where I'm gonna get milk now. Julian told me the new owners of the Casts' farm aren't even selling milk—"

"You spoke to him?" Wineke asked, eyebrow raising.

"Briefly." Lillie avoided her gaze. "It wasn't productive."

"He's an idiot then," Wineke said with a snort. "But you said he's out a dairy supplier, too? Does that strike you as odd?"

Lillie clicked her tongue. "Maybe. Or maybe Mr. Globe's trying to drive us both out of business." She sighed. "I hate the idea of not buying from Kristin anymore."

"Well, maybe Greeley will find another explanation for the poison," Wineke said. "And in the meantime, maybe Reginald could help you get more milk from somewhere farther out."

"For a price," Lillie reminded her. "Which is his right, of course. And I'd never ask for anything for free. But when I'm already trying to save money..."

"I get it," Wineke said.

"I wish we could find a mage to expedite Kristin's healing," Lillie said. "That's really how this whole mess started. She never would've let a subpar product leave her booth. Never would've stood for her sisters poisoning me." She paused, thinking back on the conversation. "Except she didn't believe me. Said there had to be another explanation. But the facts are the facts."

"The facts are the facts," Wineke agreed. "But what are you going to do about it? Take them to Sheriff Juno?"

Lillie didn't want to. There was a good chance the sheriff wouldn't believe her in the first place (though it was hard to argue with an entire room of people getting sick and an apothecary with evidence). But even though it was clear the Honeygolds were the source, Lillie couldn't do that to Kristin.

"Perhaps, with time, they'll come clean about what they did," Lillie said after a moment. "Kristin's probably getting the truth out of Esmerelda and Charla now. I'm sure they'll be at the election tonight, so maybe they'll confess."

"And if they don't?"

Lillie exhaled. "I'll travel all the way back to Pigsend for milk if I have to."

"Let's hope it doesn't come to that," Wineke said with a chuckle. "It's a shame Mr. Abora's probably going to lose, though."

"You think?"

"Kathryn's terrifying. Would you want to vote against her candidate?" Wineke asked. "And you know, Mr. Abora might not get that grant from the king's folks to double the size of the dock."

"He might not," Lillie conceded. "But doubling the size of the dock and giving it all to Mr. Globe doesn't sound much better." She sighed. "I know the McTavishes are worried. Jarvis might actually have a shot at winning this year, too. It would put a lot of power back into Mr. Globe's hands."

"Do you think we'll ever be rid of him?" Wineke said. "He was a lot nicer when his wife was around, I'll tell you that."

"Really?" Lillie quirked a brow.

"I mean, he wasn't *nice*, but he certainly didn't have this ever-present need to buy and control everything. They were more your stereotypical rich people who lived on a hill, away from the rabble. Now it feels like he's trying to buy up the entire country before someone else does."

Lillie made a thoughtful noise. "Not that I'm *ever* on his side, but the loss of his wife was probably pretty hard on him. I get the sense he's still not convinced the queen's gone, and he's doing whatever he can to keep his family safe."

"At the expense of the rest of us, I'm sure," Wineke said. "You don't have to be nice to him, you know. Even if he is your future father-in-law."

Lillie's head whipped around. "That's not happening."

"Isn't it?"

*This was a mistake.* "Absolutely not. Julian can stay on his side of the world for all I care."

"If you say so." Wineke gave her a sideways look.

Lillie was saved from the conversation when the little bell over the door jingled.

"Mr…Abora," she said, blinking at Wineke. "What are you doing here?"

The assistant mayor wore a wide (and somewhat suspiciously cheery) smile. "Ms. Sloos, Ms. Dean. Good afternoon. Mr. Sloos told me I could find you over here, Wineke. I wondered if you had a moment to chat."

Wineke's expression soured. "Shouldn't you be at the town hall? The election's starting in a few hours. Probably need to get your banners hung and whatever else someone actually running needs to do."

"Yes, well, that's why I wanted to talk." He came

up next to Wineke, still wearing that politically laced grin. "I'm so sorry you've had to drop out."

"Mm. I'm sure you are," Wineke said with a sideways glance at Lillie.

"Well, I can't say I'm not pleased to have one less opponent in the race, but I really do think more candidates make us all better," he said. "Specifically, it's forcing me to really think about my platform, and what I can do to bring the town together. I thought I was doing an adequate job, but—"

Lillie couldn't help a snort. "Sorry," she said when Mr. Abora frowned at her. "Something caught in my throat."

"I'm not pleased that Ms. Harkness is throwing her opinions around where they aren't welcome," he continued. "And I'm sorry that your speech didn't go as planned last night. It's clear you worked very hard on it and—"

"Get to the point," Wineke said, waving him off.

"Right. Well, I wanted to ask for your endorsement."

Lillie hadn't been expecting *that*—and neither had Wineke. "My...what?" Wineke asked.

Mr. Abora grinned. "You've got a great rapport with the magical folks on this side of town, and I know many of them were planning to vote for you. I think it would be an excellent show of unity if you could throw your support behind my campaign."

Wineke considered him for a moment. "And why should I? What have you done to support the magical folks?"

"I mean, I found them all storefronts and homes," Mr. Abora said. "And once I'm *officially* mayor, I'll have a lot more leeway to do more. And, well, not to cast aspersions on my opponent, but I don't think Mr. Globe's candidate is going to be a better pick."

"You have to admit he has a point," Lillie said, earning a scowl from Wineke. "And with you out of the race, the magical folks might be split. The fisherfolk certainly will be, what with Kathryn's performance last night."

"Mr. Globe certainly got his money's worth out of her." He chuckled nervously. "Well, it's your vote and your voice, so I won't keep you or belabor the point. But do know that if I get your endorsement, the assistant mayor job is open."

"You'd hire me as assistant mayor?" Wineke didn't look too upset about that.

He nodded. "It would be nice, I think, to have a magical person to help me see all sides of the issues. And it would help with that unity thing I've been working on." He cleared his throat. "The position is part-time, of course, but—"

Before he could say another word, the door to

the bakery swung open, and Kathryn barged inside, nearly shoving Mr. Abora in the process. "Hello, there, Wineke. Lovely afternoon, isn't it? Mind if we have a chat?"

Lillie couldn't help but notice that Kathryn knew Wineke's name now. "Go on, Wineke. Holler if you need me to rescue you."

"Will do," Wineke said coolly as she opened the door to the bakery. "If you please, Ms. Harkness."

Which left Lillie and Mr. Abora in the bakery alone.

"While I have you," Lillie said softly, "I wanted to apologize again for what happened the night before last. It appears someone's been lacing my milk with something awful."

"Your milk?" He blinked. "You buy from Honeygold, right?"

"How'd you know?"

"As I recall, I'm the one who introduced your dear aunt, if memory serves?" He blinked, remembering. "Grandmother?"

"Friend." Lillie tilted her head. "You introduced Etheldra to Kristin when I first moved to town?"

"I introduced her to all the merchants," he said. "She rather insisted, but it was a good idea. But back to what you were saying—the Honeygolds sold you poisoned milk?"

"That's what it appears," Lillie said. "And I

don't think there's another dairy farm around here."

"Not with the Casts selling their farm, no," Mr. Abora said with a shake of his head. "Well, not to throw my campaign in the mix, but if I'm re-elected—or elected, I should say—I promise to help you get to the bottom of things. At the very least, you should tell Juno."

"Do you think she'd do anything?"

"I think she would, yes." He nodded. "Especially if the mayor tells her to."

Lillie surveyed him, wondering if this was yet another politician's promise or the real deal. "Did you really mean it when you promised Wineke the assistant mayor position?"

He nodded. "It's vacant. We have the funds for a part-time position, so she could still work in the apothecary most of the time. And for what it's worth, she's the kind of person to solve problems." He chuckled. "Honestly, if I hadn't known you were so busy here at the bakery, I might've offered the job to you, Ms. Dean."

"I can't imagine Mr. Globe would've appreciated that," Lillie said.

"No, he wouldn't." He surveyed her. "You know, I'm honestly a little surprised no one's mentioned the blackmail letters. That seems the sort of thing Kathryn would've sniffed out and used against me. Not that she needed any help with those around the town square, mind you, but… I suppose I would've thought you'd mentioned it to her. Perhaps to bolster Wineke's campaign."

"To be honest, it never crossed my mind. You didn't send those letters to be malicious. You got in over your head—it happens a lot more than you think. We all deserve a little grace from time to time." She glanced behind her at the bakery. "To be honest, this latest round of problems has almost sent me back to Pigsend with all the damage it's done to my savings. And for what?" She crossed her arms over her chest. "Because I help people? Because I made sure that the right thing was done? Because Mr. Globe's getting fewer gold coins every month?"

Mr. Abora was quiet for a moment. "You know, you still owe me a refund for the other day."

*Really?* Lillie scowled.

"But instead of a refund…" He sighed, like he was about to do something unpleasant. "Are you absolutely, positively sure you know that the milk was the problem?"

"Yes," she said. "Greeley tested everything else I had on hand. The flour is fine, as is the sugar."

"Can you make something without milk?"

She thumbed toward the back room. "I've got a batch of macarons about ready to go in the oven. I'm using a jelly filling, so there's no milk or butter anywhere in them."

He sighed. "Then why don't you bring those down to the town hall for me? I'll serve them at my victory party." He grimaced. "Assuming I have one."

"Are you serious?" Lillie's heart beat faster. "Really? You're… I mean, I understand if you're hesitant, but—"

"As you said, we could all use a little grace sometimes." He looked toward Lillie's shared wall with the Slooses. "Do you think Wineke will endorse me, or do you think Kathryn will convince her to endorse Clancy?" He sounded a lot less nervous, and a lot more resigned.

Lillie bit her lip. "Her disgust for Mr. Globe runs deep. Kathryn would have to promise her the moon and the stars for her to even consider it—and even then, it would be a rather large ask. If I were a betting pobyd, I'd say you probably have her vote." She paused, thinking. "And for what it's worth, you have mine as well."

He smiled. "Thanks, Lillie. I'll see you down at the town hall."

"Well, I can tell you I'm absolutely *not* endorsing Clancy," Wineke said as she walked through the bakery doors. "Good*ness,* I couldn't get that woman out of the shop fast enough."

"Has she been over there all this time?" Lillie asked with a smile. The macarons had finished baking, and she was slathering jam onto each half before sandwiching them together. "What did Kathryn promise you if you endorsed Clancy?"

"Oh, she said Mr. Globe would evict Zena and let us back into our old shop," Wineke said with a laugh.

"Really?" Lillie was very surprised by that. "She must be worried, then. That's a pretty big incentive for you."

"Maybe it would've been a few months ago," Wineke said. "But I've really grown to love our shop and location here. I mean, I'm right next to you, first of all. Reginald's a few steps away. Haruko's across the street. The wharf market isn't far. And, especially after all we've endured, it feels nice to have a fresh start."

Lillie smiled. "So you're going to endorse Mr. Abora?"

"I'm voting for him," Wineke said. "But I fear Kathryn might curse my hair dye if I publicly endorsed anyone but Clancy."

"I don't think she's capable of that," Lillie said. "But perhaps it's wise not to enrage Mr. Globe more than we already have. And you don't have to publicly endorse Mr. Abora to tell people who you're voting for."

"Exactly. And, I don't know..." She shook her head. "The assistant mayor job is tempting, but I'd rather get it because I earned it, not because it was a quid pro quo. I'll talk to Mr. Abora about it after the election. If it's still available, I might consider it. Especially part-time." She glanced back at the apothecary wall. "Greeley wasn't *really* happy about the idea of me being completely gone."

"I think it would be a happy medium, then," Lillie said. "And for the record, I think you'd be great at it. Not only because I want someone in my corner when things get crazy."

"These look scrumptious," Wineke said, picking up one of the already-made cookies. "Can I try one?"

Lillie hesitated. She was confident in her bakes, and in Greeley, but she still nursed a small amount of worry that something would go wrong. But before she could stop her, Wineke popped one into her mouth.

"Outrageous," she said. "What is that? Strawberry?"

Over the next hour, Lillie watched the clock like a hawk—not only because she was counting down until the election, but because she was waiting for a reaction. Wineke, of course, was oblivious to Lillie's concern as she helped stick the macaron halves together, chatting about this, that, and the other. After half an hour, the knot in Lillie's stomach lessened, and as they finished packing up the boxes, it finally relented completely.

"Thank goodness," Lillie whispered to herself.

"Well, shall we?" Wineke asked. "It's about time for everything to get started. Let's head next door and get my beloved partner."

But Greeley was too engrossed in his

experiments on the milk. "I've got half an hour until this sets," he told them both, wearing thick goggles and gloves. "But does it matter if I vote? You're not running."

"Yes, but we need to make sure Mr. Globe's guy doesn't win," Wineke said. "Where's Fawn?"

"Doing some research on the pernicula flower at the magical tomes shop with Tom," Greeley said, turning back to stare at the vial of milk held aloft over a small flame.

When he said no more, Wineke rolled her eyes and motioned for them to leave. "He'll be along in a minute. The election is open for two hours after the speeches. I'll come back to grab him."

Together, Wineke and Lillie walked up the road toward the town hall, and they were soon joined by a stream of others. Haruko and Reginald, who were feeling better and no longer spurting magic everywhere, were already in the square with Edwina and Mattea, a small, squatty witch.

"I heard you found the source of that strange sickness," Reginald said. "Greeley said someone was sabotaging your bakery."

"It's true," Lillie said. "Apparently triggered by magic. I had no idea, because it doesn't affect pobyds. I feel awful about what happened the other day."

Reginald waved her off. "No lasting harm done.

I was able to pop back up to the town hall and fix all the things we, erm, charred."

"Are those macarons?" Edwina asked, peering into the box.

"Are they safe to eat?" Reginald asked warily.

"Oh, Reginald, don't be silly. I had two about an hour ago." Wineke waved him off. "The problem was in the milk, and macarons are happily dairy-free."

"Besides that," Lillie said, grateful for the vote of confidence from Wineke, "these are for Mr. Abora's victory party." She shifted, glancing at Wineke. "He's got my vote."

"Hear, hear," Haruko said with a nod. "Ours too."

The sentiment was echoed by the others as well, and for the first time, it seemed Mr. Abora might not be out of the running.

The town hall was already packed with people, so Lillie and the rest had to stand at the back of the room. Instinctively, Lillie scanned the room for Julian, finding him sitting with Noemi and the rest of the transplants near Clancy. Thankfully, Mr. Globe hadn't arrived yet. Lillie was hoping to avoid him altogether.

At the front left of the room, Mr. Abora stood by himself, wringing his hands and looking a little nervous. On the opposite side, Clancy, Jarvis, and

Kathryn waited, the latter looking bored. The McTavishes hadn't arrived, but there were more than a few fisherfolk in attendance.

"I don't think I've ever seen so many people in here," Wineke said. "Not even when Mr. Abora was divvying up the homes to people. Remember that?"

"We weren't up here yet," Reginald said.

"Ah, well, it was tense. Then Julian Globe got up and took a slice of Lillie's cake and ate it." She wagged her brows at Lillie. "It was *very* attractive."

Lillie's treacherous gaze found Julian again. Thankfully, his back was to her. "Was it? Just seemed like a nice thing to do. A vote of confidence."

"Maybe he should do that to your macarons," Wineke said with a wink.

Lillie was saved from answering by Mr. Abora coming to the center of the room and clapping his hands. "Good evening, everyone. Thank you for coming to the Silverkeep mayoral election. A special welcome to those of you also here for the Fisherfolk Council election, too. I know it's a bit unconventional to have two elections at the same time, but it's less work for everyone involved."

"Speak for yourself," Juno growled behind him. "I've got two rounds of ballots to count."

"Right. Well, I suppose we should get on with it." Mr. Abora picked up a slip of paper. "Everyone intending to cast their vote for mayor can come up to the front and grab one of these. Write your preferred candidate on it—"

"That's C-A-S-T," Kathryn prompted with a grin and a wink.

"Erm, yes." Mr. Abora adjusted his shirt. "And when you've finished, fold the paper in half and put it in the box. If you're also voting in the Fisherfolk Council, the McTavishes have a set of papers for their election. I believe those are yellow."

Jan McTavish stood up in the front of the room, waving a stack of yellow parchment.

"At seven o'clock on the dot," Mr. Abora continued, "Sheriff Juno will count the ballots for the Fisherfolk Council first, then the mayoral race," Mr. Abora finished. "Good luck to all the candidates. Now, if you'll line up in the center of the room, we'll start handing out ballots."

"Wait, wait," Kathryn said. "You've forgotten that the Fisherfolk candidates are giving their endorsements for each of the mayoral candidates."

"Right, how could I forget?" The look on Mr. Abora's face made it clear he *hadn't* forgotten, and had hoped he could get away with not mentioning it. "McTavishes? Why don't you go first."

Orxan stood up and looked out across the room. Lillie followed his gaze and counted most, if not all, of the fisherfolk in attendance.

"Jan and I would like to offer our endorsement

to Mr. Abora," he said, earning an unabashed sigh of relief from the current assistant mayor. "We think he has the best chance of making things better than they are, and at this point, keeping a steady hand on the leadership of Silverkeep is essential. Now's not the time to be putting new people in charge."

"Okay, this isn't *your* campaign speech," Kathryn barked. "Jarvis?"

Jarvis stood up. "Clancy."

He sat.

"Short, sweet, and succinct," Kathryn said. "Exactly how the people like it. Now, why don't we get this thing on the road, eh? I've got places to be, and I am *absolutely* leaving the moment the clock strikes seven." She laughed, but Lillie was quite sure she wasn't joking.

It was a very slow but orderly process. Some people had taken their ballot to mark elsewhere, but others seemed to know exactly who they were voting for and did it quickly. Lillie and the others queued up, and within twenty minutes, they'd reached the front of the line.

"Would you like to cast a ballot for the fisherfolk election?" Jan asked Lillie, holding a piece of yellow parchment.

"I probably shouldn't," Lillie said. "It doesn't feel right to weigh in. But I do hope the two of you win. You've done a good job."

Jan thanked her and instead handed the blank piece of yellow paper to Hipolita, who was right behind her. Lillie took the blank white sheet from Juno, who barely gave her a glance.

"C'mon," Wineke said, eyeing Kathryn, who was glaring at her. "Let's do this somewhere more private."

They found a spot on an empty bench, and Lillie and Wineke both scribbled the name *Kemp Abora* on their sheets before walking back up to the front to the waiting ballot box.

"Thank you for keeping an eye on things," Wineke said diplomatically to Juno.

"Someone has to ensure there's no hanky-panky," Juno said as Lillie dropped her slip of paper into the box. "Seems like there's been a bit of that lately. Heard someone was making people sick." She eyed Lillie. "Something you want to tell me, Ms. Dean?"

"Not at the moment, no." Lillie forced a smile. "But if that changes, I'll certainly let you know."

"I'm sorry to hear you've dropped out of the campaign," Juno said to Wineke. "But it can be hard to run against people who have lots of money."

Wineke gave a brief smile as she dropped her ballot in. "Thanks. Suppose I'll have to work to make things better for the world in other ways."

"Sometimes that's the most effective way."

Lillie turned to leave, only to find herself face to face with Julian. He watched her with something unreadable in his gaze, and she stared wordlessly at him for probably longer than was polite.

"Can I cast my vote?" he asked.

"Right. Yes. Sorry." Lillie quickly scampered around him, refusing to look back and give the rest of the town more gossip fodder.

"I suppose I should go get my partner before he falls into the milk," Wineke said with a sigh. "Are you gonna stick around?"

"I think so," Lillie said, finding a spot in the back and doing her best to ignore Julian walking out the door. "Not as if there's anything else to do right now."

She watched the procession, mentally trying to decide who'd vote for whom. Jeremias was clearly a vote for Mr. Abora and the McTavishes, because he nodded at them as he left. May Janik, another merchant, was for Clancy. Zena was for Clancy, obviously, as was Perry Buhlman—who made sails—Maire Gaides, and Jessup Overman, the cobbler. Edwina, Haruko, Reginald, and Mattea were for Mr. Abora.

Mr. Globe sauntered in, his dark shoes clacking on the floor. He'd already filled out his ballots, so he handed them over, then turned to walk out without another word.

Except, of course, he spotted Lillie and made a beeline for her instead.

"Great," Lillie muttered under her breath.

"Ms. Dean, I hear you're having trouble with your bakery again," he said.

"Yes, funny how that keeps happening," Lillie replied mildly. "Though this time, it does feel rather personal, considering someone's used a poison that's triggered by magic."

"As I'm sure Ms. Sloos can tell you, that's more common than you think," Mr. Globe said, his expression inscrutable. "A pobyd's magic is quite powerful when used in certain ways, isn't it?"

Lillie sensed he was trying to hint at something, perhaps her history in Lower Pigsend, but she wasn't going to take the bait. "Well, I'm grateful we have an answer so I can get back to baking and doing what I do best. It's a good thing I'm stubborn, or someone might convince me to close up shop." She met his gaze with a challenge. "Which, I'm happy to report, I will never do."

"Indeed." He nodded. "Have a good night."

Lillie watched him go, frowning. That was, perhaps, the strangest interaction she'd ever had with Julian's father. And it told her exactly nothing.

As the first of the two hours of open voting elapsed, some of the farmers arrived, including a pair of smartly dressed people who nodded to the

Casts. Perhaps the new owners of their farm? The Honeygolds, too, came, though Kristin wasn't with them. Lillie carefully watched their interaction with Kathryn, who kept checking her timepiece. Either she was doing a very good job of pretending she had no idea who they were, or…she didn't.

Charla and Esmerelda cast their ballots and turned, immediately spotting Lillie in the back. They had a quick argument that Lillie couldn't hear, then approached with their heads held high.

"We will *thank you* to stop spreading rumors about our farm," Charla said. "We have nothing to do with your bakery's problems."

"The apothecary—"

"That awful, *rude* man who came by three times today?" Esmerelda huffed. "Asking us all manner of questions about our fields, what we grow, where it is?" She sniffed. "It's bad enough we had to deal with you, but now we're having to field questions from people asking if our butter is safe to consume."

Lillie's brow furrowed. "You haven't had any complaints, have you?"

"As a matter of fact…" Esmerelda swallowed, looking at Charla. "We have. Today. One of our usual customers said she was out sick all day yesterday."

"You're joking." Lillie straightened. "Did they buy—"

"The butter you made for me." Esmerelda's chin lifted. "I don't know why you're trying to ruin our family's business. I know Charla and I haven't been very nice to you in the past, but—"

"Me? I'm not trying to... You're the one poisoning *my* milk!" Lillie said. "Well, maybe not you, but the milk is poisoned. Greeley's confirming it."

"We've sold jugs of milk to people with absolutely no problem. But the butter?"

Lillie had no idea what to say. She'd been so convinced someone was out to get her, but what if they weren't?

"I hear you've got money coming in," Lillie said to Esmerelda. "Something about a big windfall. I'm sure the closing of my business was essential to that deal. Mr. Globe won't be pleased to—"

"Mr. Globe?" Esmerelda blanched.

"Essi, what is she talking about?" Charla asked. "What windfall?"

Esmerelda glared at Lillie before turning to her wife. "I'd heard the king was giving money to people whose lives and businesses were disrupted by the queen. I... I applied for some since we'd lost our tanddaes. The amount would be enough to cover the repairs to the house and buy some more livestock."

Charla swallowed. "Why didn't you tell me?"

"You wanted us to sell," Esmerelda said. "I know it's hard for you to be there. But I couldn't... That's our home, Char. It's where we got married. I can't imagine being or doing anything else." She took Charla's hand. "I want to save our home."

Charla kissed Esmerelda's knuckles. "I know, dear. I just don't want to see you so worried about it."

"If this does what it's supposed to, we won't have to worry." Esmerelda looked up at Lillie. "Assuming nobody spreads any nasty rumors about our business."

Lillie shook her head, chastened. "Then where did the poison come from?"

"I have no idea, Ms. Dean, but perhaps you should consider that one of your mousy friends might not be so trustworthy," Charla said. "Goodness knows Zena told us all about Fawn and her perfidy. Maybe she's the one poisoning you."

"I'll keep that in mind," Lillie said quietly. "Thanks."

"So these are the Honeygolds?" Kathryn's nasally voice broke through Lillie's reverie. "As I said, never met 'em before in my life." She surveyed Charla, who surveyed her right back. "Right? Tell this ridiculous woman we've never met."

"I'm sure I'd remember you," Charla said dryly.

"I've seen you at Jarvis's booth," Esmerelda

replied. "But no, we've never met."

"Great. Now." Kathryn crooked her finger at Lillie. "I need to have a word with you. Outside. Right now."

"If there's one thing I hate, it's someone having incorrect information about me," Kathryn said, throwing her hair behind her head as she and Lillie stepped outside. "And you've been glaring at me all night, so before I officially clock out and hop on the first wagon to a real town, I need you to understand some facts."

Lillie crossed her arms expectantly.

"Number one: I'm not poisoning anyone. If I was going to run you out of business, I would do it much less overtly. Poisoning is gross."

Lillie shifted. Julian had said the same thing.

"Number two: I've never met the Honeygolds, as we've established."

"What about their sister Kristin?" Lillie asked pointedly.

"Who?" Kathryn quirked a brow. "I haven't. That's the truth. No idea who they are or what they do. I assume they shovel manure or something, based on how they were dressed."

"You convinced the Casts to sell their farm," Lillie said, ignoring the dig. "They're neighbors."

"I'm sorry, have you *been* out there? Neighbor is a very loose term." She chuckled. "If they're neighbors, so are you and Julian."

Lillie pursed her lips. Fair point.

"And for the record, I didn't have to do much convincing. Prunella and Clancy were already getting offers from spellworkers. Something about their farm having lots of latent magic in the ground, great for growing the kinds of herbs that are now in high demand in King's' Capital. Don't feel too bad for them. They got a *great* deal."

"Prunella didn't seem happy with the arrangement. She thought they'd sell and leave Silverkeep, not stick around."

"Well, I might've told a small white lie there." She shrugged. "Audo was fine with them selling the farm, but he didn't want them to leave-leave. This town without a butcher? Probably wouldn't do so well. Audo's been searching for someone to take their place, but hasn't been successful yet. Luckily, I don't think it'll be a problem, because his butcher's not going to have a new job tomorrow."

"You don't think Clancy's going to win?" Lillie asked. "Isn't that what you were paid to accomplish?"

"I did what I was paid to do," she said evasively. "Which was run an *amazing* campaign in under a week. The fact that Clancy's going to get half the vote is a miracle. A well-paid-for miracle, mind you, but a miracle."

Lillie shook her head, annoyance blossoming in her chest. Kathryn was making a *lot* of sense, but it didn't explain the source of the poison.

"Now, to the *real* reason you've got a vendetta against me," Kathryn said with a knowing smile. "Julian."

Heat flared into Lillie's cheeks. "There's not… There's nothing—"

"You can keep saying that, but nobody believes you. At least four people in this town have bets on when you're going to give in and make bakery babies."

Lillie coughed. She *really* hoped that didn't get back to Mr. Globe.

"I won't lie. Audo invited me not only for my political prowess, but because he was hoping I might be able to rekindle something with his son so he'd stop giving you the lovesick schoolboy eyes." She shrugged. "Why Audo hates you so much, I haven't a clue."

"Don't you?"

"He didn't share it with me." She waved her off. "Anyway, I gave it my best shot, but Julian has eyes for one gal, and it sure ain't me."

*This was a mistake.* "I'm sure that's not true."

"Well, you're not paying me to tell you the truth, so I really don't care if you believe me or not." She laughed. "But if I were you, I'd stop looking at this poisoning thing with the thought that someone's out to get you. You might actually see what's going on."

"Yeah? And what's that?"

"Hear me out," Kathryn continued. "You think Mr. Globe's out to destroy your business, right? That he hates you *so* much that he'd hire someone like me to sneak around and lace your milk with magic, hurting the people of this town—perhaps even his own daughter, if she happened to eat one of your pastries—just to get you to leave?"

Lillie considered the question—really considered it. It had seemed the obvious answer, of course, but looking at it objectively... But what other explanation could there be?

Kathryn sighed as if this were painfully obvious

to her. "Tell me where you've found this poison."

"In my pastries," Lillie said. "From the milk that came from Honeygold Farms."

"And was it only your milk that was poisoned?"

Lillie opened her mouth to respond but stopped. "N-no. Esmerelda said butter I'd churned for her to sell had made their customers sick, too."

"So the only connection is—"

"That my magic was involved," Lillie said. "Are you saying—"

"I'm saying that the new owners of the Casts' farm are planting all kinds of magical plants next door. Maybe something blew into the…I don't know, sheep? I have no clue what they raise there." She shrugged. "Perhaps nobody's out to get you at all, and it's one big coincidence."

Lillie couldn't find words.

Yet the puzzle pieces fell into place, finally making sense after the last bit of information came to light. The Casts had sold their farm to someone who was growing ingredients for potions. They'd recently planted a great number of new things—Kristin had mentioned offhand that the cows had "gotten into the wrong field" again.

Was it truly that simple?

Kathryn pushed her bag up onto her shoulder as she checked her timepiece again. "Don't worry, sweetie. I won't charge you my usual rate for advice.

Consider this one a personal favor from someone who has similar taste in men." She closed the timepiece. "Seven. Finally. Do you know where I could get a horse or a wagon or even a winged beast? At this point, I am *not* picky."

"You aren't sticking around for the results?" Lillie asked. "Mr. Globe might not pay you if your candidates don't win."

"Who do you think I am?" Kathryn laughed. "I was very clear in my retainer that I would only work the election. What the masses decide is none of my concern. I told Audo he had an uphill climb, and I never make guarantees."

"You told Clancy *and* Jarvis that you had it in the bag," Lillie said.

"I never make guarantees to the people who hire me." She winked. "Very important distinction. Now, if you don't mind, I've got to find someone who can get me *out* of this fish-smelling town to somewhere with a decent bottle of wine."

~

The town hall was completely full without a place for anyone to sit. At the front of the room, Juno was counting votes, murmuring to herself as she wrote on the paper. The two sets of candidates sat nervously on either side, waiting for the results.

Esmerelda and Charla were in the middle of the room, too far in for Lillie to get to them easily. She was buzzing with this new thought—this idea that maybe, *maybe* the answer was simple. She'd almost certainly burned her bridge with them, even with Kristin's friendship, but she owed it to them to give them an explanation, at least.

Unfortunately, before Lillie could make her way over to them, Juno cleared her throat and announced she had the results.

"First up, the Fisherfolk Council elections," she said. "By my count, we have Jarvis Collin with sixteen votes, and the McTavishes at sixteen."

The room went silent, the fisherfolk staring at each other with shock clear on their faces.

"And for the mayoral election," Juno continued, looking grim. "We also have a tie."

"Well, what in the world does that mean?" Jarvis said. "Who won?"

"Nobody did," Juno said. "Unless there's anyone in the room who hasn't voted yet?"

As if summoned by the words, the back doors opened, and to Lillie's utter surprise, Kristin came hobbling in on her crutches, her leg bound. She was dripping with sweat and seemed to need a minute to catch her breath.

"What in the world?" Esmerelda barked, standing up and making her way over. "Kristin Honeygold, do *not* tell me you walked the whole way here."

"Are you nuts? Of course I took the wagon." She laughed. "But it's still a long way from where I left it to here." She turned to Lillie with a smile. "I have great news for you. I figured out what happened."

"Your neighbors planted something?" Lillie suggested.

"Yeah. Remember I said Charla let the cows eat in the wrong field? Well, turns out it was covered in purple flowers—"

"The pernicula flower!" Greeley popped up from the audience, rushing over. "I had a hunch. I tested three bottles from the Honeygolds. They *all* had the poison in them!"

"Preposterous," Esmerelda said. "The pobyd clearly—"

"The poison's coming from the cows," Kristin said. "Those purple flowers that I *told* you were weird-looking, remember? The cows are eating them, ingesting the poison, and it's coming out in the milk."

"And we're only seeing it when I use pobyd magic on them," Lillie finished.

Esmerelda and Charla stared at each other wordlessly. Kristin smirked, and Greeley looked like he'd won first prize in a contest.

"So how do we fix it?" Lillie asked. "I can't bake with poisoned milk."

"That's what Fawn was going to check," Greeley

said. "And why I was late. There's a tincture we can add to the milk to neutralize the poison until it's clear from the cows' systems. I tried it myself." He gestured to his stomach. "It works great."

Lillie could've cried, except... "I don't know if your sisters will still sell to me. I really did make a mess of things." She turned to Charla and Esmerelda. "I'm so very sorry."

"No, they're the ones who should be apologizing!" Kristin said hotly. "Acting like you're some kind of pariah because you have magic. And even worse, you two let those cows eat in that field, even though I *told* you those flowers looked dodgy. You know better than that. Remember a few years ago when the tanddaes got into that patch of mushrooms, and we had to sell orange wool?" She shook her head. "I break my leg, and everything goes to pot."

The wives shared a bashful look. "I won't lie," Charla said quietly. "I wasn't too unhappy to hear you might be leaving town. We should've... I mean, I didn't know, but we should've looked a little harder at our own backyard once you told us the milk was poisoned. Instead of just...kicking you out."

"Agreed," Esmerelda said, her cheeks flushing.

"Great, now can we all stop being at each other's throats?" Kristin said, adjusting herself on her crutches. "Lillie needs butter and eggs. We need to *sell* butter alongside our milk."

"Even if we go back to selling to Lillie, it's not going to be enough," Charla said. "We're barely making ends meet as it is, and there's no guarantee we'll get this grant."

"Julian." The word came to Lillie before she could stop herself. She turned toward the crowd, who was watching them intently. "Is Julian here?"

He rose, wearing the same white shirt she'd seen him in earlier and looking too handsome for words. He crossed the room quickly, joining the huddle at the back of the town hall. Lillie forced herself to look neutral as he approached, even though her entire body electrified at his closeness.

"You were getting milk from the Casts, right?" Lillie said. "And now you're having to go out of town?"

"Yeah."

"Absolutely not," Kristin said with a shake of her head. "He already asked and I told him no. We're team Pobyd Perfections. I refuse to sell to a Globe."

"You should, because he needs it—and you could use the extra money," Lillie said, ignoring the sight out of the corner of her eye of Julian smiling. "Once we sort out the issue with the milk, of course. But there's no reason you shouldn't conduct business with him. We're..." She exhaled, looking out at the very interested crowd. "We're one town. We help each other. And I think it's silly that you both have a need the other could meet."

"Are you sure, Lillie?" Kristin said, more under her breath than to Julian. "I really don't mind telling him to kick rocks."

"Yes." Lillie finally forced herself to look at Julian, whose entire existence was enough to take her breath away. "I think that would be beneficial to all of us."

"Thanks, Lillie," he whispered.

*Lillie.* She tried not to take that personally.

"Fine." Kristin shifted on her crutches. "Come to the farm tomorrow, *Mr. Globe*, and we'll sort out the details." She glanced at Charla and Esmerelda. "Since I can't trust you two not to ruin things, apparently."

Someone cleared their throat behind the group, and all heads turned to find Sheriff Juno waiting with two pieces of paper.

"If you three are done discussing all the things wrong with this town and how to fix them," she said. "We are still in need of Ms. Honeygold's vote for the fisherfolk and the mayoral elections."

"Really?" Kristin turned to her sister. "They wouldn't let you cast a vote on my behalf?"

Esmerelda shook her head. "Juno said you had

to be here."

"Ah, well. I'm here now." She shifted. "Just put my name for Kemp Abora and the McTavishes—"

A cheering roar echoed from half the room, earning a frown from Kristin. "That's an odd way to celebrate a vote being cast."

Lillie laughed. "I've got a lot to fill you in on."

"Oh, yeah," Greeley said, plucking one of the purple flowers from the field. "That's exactly what it is. Right, Fawn?"

"Mm." The mouse hopped off Greeley's shoulder and tore the flower petals in half. "Absolutely."

"So how are we gonna prevent this from happening again?" Kristin said to her sisters.

"I've spoken with Feliciano—he owns the farm next door now," Esmerelda said. "They feel awful. They hadn't meant to plant those so close to the cow pastures, but apparently, the flowers are quick to bloom, and the seeds spread too far. But as long as the cows graze on the southern fields until we can get these sorted, it should be fine."

"Well, they're relatively easy to get rid of," Tom said, kneeling on the ground. "You just want to seed the field with fescue, which will grow taller than the flowers, eat up all the nutrients, and block out the sun. And bonus, it'll be delicious for the cows, too. Maybe three to four weeks, and you can set the cows loose out here again."

"And in the meantime," Greeley said, "I can leave you with the tincture to test the milk for any lingering effects. It'll turn the liquid blue if there's any trace of the poison. And, of course, if it does turn blue, I've got the other tincture to neutralize it."

"Wonderful," Kristin said. "Julian was very clear he wanted us to make sure there wasn't anything in his milk, even though he doesn't have any magic. He's expecting his first delivery in the morning."

Lillie forced herself to look neutral. "He already came by?"

"Early. He's up at dawn, just like you," Kristin said. "You know, I rather underestimated him. He's very cordial and nice and respectful. Very grateful to do business with us, too. I practically raked him over the coals with what I'm charging him." She winked at Lillie. "Still team Pobyd Perfections. And he doesn't make our butter, so he gets to pay the full price for his milk."

"I think that's more than fair," Lillie said with a sad smile. "I'm glad things are working out for everyone."

~

Back at the Pobyd Perfections Bakery, Lillie got straight to work. First thing, she made a sign promising all ingredients had been cleared by Sloos apothecary next door. Then she started with chocolate chip cookies, muffins, scones, a large lemon cake, and—just because she was feeling happy—a double batch of macarons.

"Lillie! You're back!" Ursil cheered as he walked inside with Jan and Orxan in tow. "Look at all this!"

"And safe to eat," Lillie said. "We found the source of the problem."

"Everyone in town heard," Orxan said with a laugh. "Do remind me to thank Kristin Honeygold when she's feeling better. Could you imagine if we had to vote *again*?"

Lillie grinned. "Outrageous."

"Is that a lemon cake I see?" Jan asked, peering over the case.

"Made especially for you," Lillie said, reaching for her cake cutter. "I thought you might want a celebratory treat."

"Ah, well." Jan shared a look with Orxan. "You

don't really have to do that anymore."

"No?"

"At Orxan's urging, I went to speak with the apothecaries and the mage," they said. "I don't exactly want fairy dust everywhere I walk, but I'm ready to be less...reticent about my lineage. Greeley said he'll make me a tincture that'll help keep the mess at bay while allowing some of my magic to come out."

Lillie's heart swelled. "That's wonderful. And no more iron powder."

"No more iron powder." They smiled as if it were the most wonderful thing in the world. "And even better—we heard from King's Capital this morning. They've accepted Mr. Abora's request to expand the size of the dock. Reginald's going to be busy, but he says he's up to the task. We're creating three new fisherfolk slips and another space for Jeremias Scarp."

"That's wonderful! So everyone will get a spot now?"

"Jarvis can't even complain about it," Orxan said with a chuckle. "And that's rare for him."

~

The rest of the morning was surprisingly busy, with several customers, including Mr. Roudie, mentioning that the vote of confidence from Sloos apothecary was enough to get them in the door.

Lillie sold out of everything she'd baked and had to run next door to get the remaining bottles of milk Greeley had purchased the day before for the afternoon rush.

She was putting out cupcakes when Mr. Abora walked in, beaming from ear to ear. "Ms. Dean. Lovely to see you back up and running. Silverkeep is much better with your bakery in its midst."

"You already won. You don't have to keep campaigning," Lillie said with a laugh.

"Sorry. Habit. But I am pleased you're back open. And even more pleased to hear you brokered a deal for Globe Café and Honeygold Farms, too. As I understand it, Mr. Globe had thought he'd gotten the better of his son by forcing him to leave town to get his milk, but you seem to have outsmarted him."

"I don't know about that. There are probably a hundred dairy farmers around here that Julian could've bought from."

"Fifteen within a thirty-mile radius, but who's counting?" He shrugged. "The Honeygolds are the closest with the Cast farm out of business."

Lillie laughed as she leaned against the counter. "You really do have the measure of everything happening around Silverkeep, don't you?"

"I try. It's going to be interesting not having weekly meetings with Mr. Globe." He chuckled nervously. "I mean, I've already got him sending me letters, so I assume he'll want to meet. But I'm not going to let him boss me around anymore. I've got the mandate of the people, and, between you and me, he's far too entrenched in Silverkeep to really do anything drastic. So we'll just have to get along, I suppose."

*If only.* "Did you just come by to get something to eat?"

"I also wanted to thank you for those absolutely delightful macarons yesterday," he said. "They were a huge hit at my victory party. I'm planning on having a few smaller meetings in the next few weeks with some focus groups in town to hear what improvements the people want. Would you be interested in catering that for me?"

Lillie was absolutely overjoyed to accept—and the rest of the day went just as well. The Jacob twins came by after work for their evening pastry and placed a rather intricate order for a cake with honeycomb and small chocolate bees for Evangeline's birthday in a few weeks, and Mr. Roudie came in again to ask Lillie to make a couple of those love-filled cupcakes for him and Benetta.

"I told her about the Kovens being all lovey-dovey," he said. "She said she'd be into it."

Lillie told him she'd do it, but only after *she* confirmed with Benetta that it was all right.

Between them and Mr. Abora's catering orders,

her savings were filling right back up, and she was feeling optimistic again about her chances of paying off Mr. Globe's debt.

Except, of course, there was nothing waiting for her at the end of it when she did. She hadn't seen Julian since the night before. She'd been hoping to see him at Kristin's earlier, or maybe for him to pop down and have that discussion they needed to have about *the kiss*.

Then again, she'd told him there was nothing to discuss. Perhaps he was listening to her.

"You should be over the moon," Rey said as he stopped in before his nightly trek to the Silverkeep Inn. "You solved the mystery—"

"Kinda. This one was a group effort," Lillie said with a laugh. In fact, had Lillie not been blinded by her own jealousy, she might've seen the problem sooner.

"Still. All is well now. Why aren't you happy?"

"I am happy," Lillie said, though she couldn't muster a smile. "You go on and head to Lenoire's. Be sure to find out how mad Mr. Globe is that both his candidates lost."

"Oh, you know I will." He hesitated at his mousehole. "Are you sure you're all right?"

"Never better. Have a good one."

Then Lillie was alone. She tidied up the front and back rooms, made a list of all the goodies she was going to bake in the morning, and finally felt the tug of sleep coming for her. It had been a long week, and she was ready for some well-earned rest.

But before she could head upstairs, there was a soft knock at her back door.

Her breath caught. She knew who it was, just by the pattern.

Julian waited on her back step, looking disheveled and miserable. "Can I come in?"

Lillie stepped aside and let him through. He stood at a distance from her, his gaze still on the ground.

"I heard you and Kristin came to an agreement this morning," Lillie began softly. "Thank you for helping her."

"She's helping me more than I'm helping her," he said roughly. "One week of having to travel by wagon to get my wares, and I was losing my mind."

She nodded, not sure what else to say.

"Is Rey around?"

"No?" Lillie's brow furrowed. "Why?"

"I don't want us to be overheard," he said, finally meeting her gaze. There was a storm of emotion there. "Because I need to explain myself. Here. In person. Not in a letter. Not with anyone around to misconstrue what I say. You and me. Face to face. Like this."

Lillie's heart sputtered. "Okay. You've got me."

"When I said kissing you was a mistake—"

"Julian, you don't—" She turned away from him, but he took her elbow and turned her back.

"Please, Lils. I have to tell you this. Because it dawned on me that you thought I meant it was a mistake to kiss you at all," he said. "Which couldn't be further from the truth. I've wanted to kiss you since the moment you set foot in my bakery and spat out one of my overdone tarts."

She swallowed hard, lifting her chin defiantly even as a crack formed in the carefully constructed wall around her heart. "You didn't act that way when I came to the bakery to make the Kovens' cake."

He took another hesitant step closer. "Believe me, when you came to my kitchen the other night, looking desperate and worried, all I wanted to do was make you forget whatever upset you. But I was *trying* to remain cordial, seeing as we'd come to an agreement that we wouldn't pursue a relationship while your debt to my father was still outstanding. I thought we both understood that."

"But after we..." She licked her lips. "You left."

"I had to leave," he said. "Because I didn't trust myself not to kiss you until you couldn't see straight if I didn't."

Another crack. "And after I confronted Kathryn? You acted like—"

He barked a laugh. "Do you think I was about to bare my soul to you while Silverkeep's most notorious gossip was on your shoulder?" He shook his head. "The truth is I've wanted to explain myself, but I had to wait until everything died down to get you alone."

She swallowed. "You have me alone now. Explain yourself."

"I've been planning our first kiss for months," he said softly. "I wanted to make everything perfect, to bring you roses, to set the scene exactly right. For you and me to be…well, of sound mind, for lack of a better phrase. I wanted to look in your eyes and for you to know, without a shadow of a doubt, that I was kissing you because I wanted to, not because anything else was influencing me."

Lillie swallowed hard. "Oh."

"And unless I'm very much mistaken," he said, sliding closer to her and resting his palm on the small of her back, "there's no pobyd magic floating around the kitchen to influence us, is there?"

"No," Lillie said, though her heart was pounding so fast she wasn't exactly sure she was completely sane.

"So, if it's all right with you," he said, leaning in closer, "I'd very much like to redo our first kiss."

And she wanted, very much, to do that. But she couldn't open that door. Not when she'd have to slam it closed right after. "We can't, Julian. We aren't supposed to see each other right now," she whispered. "Let alone…let alone kiss. It'll just make things worse when we can't be together."

"Yes, well, I'm not sure I can survive waiting until you've paid my father back," Julian said with a wry smile. "Every time I see you, it's like a cool drink of water after I've been dying in the desert—"

"Julian, that's a bit hyperbolic," Lillie said.

"I love you, Lillie."

Lillie gasped as she took a step back. *Love?* Julian *loved* her? She could deny it, could tell herself he was kidding himself, but the emotion was clear on his face. It was the same reason memories of him had flooded her mind when she was making the Kovens' cake. But to hear him declare it so openly… she hadn't been prepared for *that*.

"Please say something," Julian whispered, not meeting her eyes. "Otherwise, one might think this feeling is unrequited."

"Are you joking?" Lillie scoffed. "The way I absolutely lost my mind when I thought Kathryn might've turned your head—"

He let out a bark of victorious laughter. "You *were* jealous."

"Of course I was jealous," Lillie said hotly. "She was quite clear about how good a kisser you are and *how* romantic, and then, to add insult to injury, she could just walk into your bakery whenever she pleased. Meanwhile, I've been down here struggling with this poisoning nonsense, and all I wanted was to talk to you, Julian. And when I thought you didn't feel the same, I've never been so heartbroken in my life." She exhaled, not sure if she was about to burst into tears or yell at him some more.

"But now that you know that you're the only one I love and want to be with," Julian said, "how do you feel now?"

The truth was as clear as day. Why else would she risk her life's work—her bakery—for a moment in his presence? The only explanation was that Lillie Dean was hopelessly, completely, and unequivocally in love with Julian Globe.

And that was the worst realization of all.

"It doesn't matter how I feel. We still have your father to contend with," she said sadly.

"I've been thinking about that," Julian whispered, cupping her cheek. She leaned into it, reveling in his touch on her skin. "If the problem is my father not knowing, then I'm pretty sure we can work around that."

Lillie wasn't going to let his sweet words addle her brain, but it was hard. "He has spies everywhere."

"Well, as I understand it," Julian continued, swaying with her ever so slightly, "I've got a new dairy supplier in Honeygold Farms, don't I?"

Lillie quirked a brow. "Yes…?"

"And, well, I'm sure that I'll have to make trips out there to inspect the product," he said.

"Do you do that now?"

"No, but I can start. Being a businessman and all." He chuckled. "And if you happen to be there checking on your dear friend Kristin's recovery…"

"There are small folk at Kristin's farm, too, you know. They talk."

"Then I'll ensure there's no one around to see us," Julian said. "Look, sneaking around isn't my preference, but if it means I get to hold you like this, I'll take what I can get."

And *oh*, she wanted to be held by him. She wanted to believe that they wouldn't get caught, that she could pay back his father, that it was all worth it, in the end.

"Meet me at Kristin's farm tomorrow after the lunch rush," Julian said, pressing his forehead to hers. "Be with me in whatever capacity you can right now. We'll work together to pay back my father. And when you're fully out from under him, I can shout it to the rooftops that you're mine."

But that wasn't the only thing Audo had hanging over Lillie's head. He also knew about her past in Lower Pigsend, and Lillie wasn't sure Julian would think so highly of her if he found out how truly villainous she could be.

"What?" Julian cupped her cheek, thumbing her skin gently. "Talk to me. You can tell me anything."

Could she, though? Could she tell him that her selfish desires had nearly caused three thousand people to be exposed to the mad queen? What would he think of her then?

She would tell him....eventually. But she was tired of all the walls and barriers and roadblocks to happiness. For now, she would kick that particular stone down the road.

"If we can keep it a secret," Lillie whispered, taking his hand off her face and kissing his knuckles, "then I'll meet you at Honeygold Farms tomorrow afternoon."

His smile was warm. "Can we redo that first kiss now?"

She didn't answer, just closed the distance between them. Their fake first kiss had been frantic and harried, but this was slow. She inhaled his scent and his taste, reveling in the way he held her. If he wanted to forget that magically induced kiss for this one...she wouldn't say no.

Because while the first kiss had been earth-shattering, this one was perfection.

Lillie continues her adventures in

# ACKNOWLEGMENTS

As always, first thanks goes to my husband, for supporting me, believing in me, and being my rock during the difficult season of two very small children and me trying to take on the world. Thanks must also go to my parents, my in-laws, and my aunt for being the world's best village and allowing me to keep writing with said very small children.

Thanks to Chelsea, Danielle, Lisa, and Lacey for being the all-star team who helps bring these beautiful books to life.

Thanks go to the Sush Street Team for being the cheerleaders who love these books and continue to read everything I put out.

# Also By The Author

## THE WEARY DRAGON INN SERIES, A COZY FANTASY SERIES

Bev may not know who she was before she showed up in the quaint village of Pigsend five years ago, but that doesn't bother her much. She's made a tidy little life for herself as the proprietor of the Weary Dragon Inn, where the most notable event is when she makes her famous rosemary bread. But when earthquakes and sinkholes start appearing all over town, including near Bev's front door, she's got to put on her sleuthing hat to figure out what—or who—might be causing them before the entire town disappears.

Drinks and Sinkholes is the first book in the Weary Dragon Inn series, and is available in ebook, physical, and audiobook at your favorite retailer.

# Also By The Author

## FIREWING INVESTIGATIONS

Dragon Shifter PJ Norris has just flunked out of university, but he's got a new task: pick up where the grannies left off and keep looking for more dragon shifters like himself. With his best friend Grant by his side, along with a new amulet that gives him more access to his dragon magic, PJ hits the road in hopes to find more shifters—and solve a few magical mysteries along the way.

PJ Norris and the Town with the Butterfly Problem is the first book in the Firewing Investigations series, and is available in ebook, physical, and audiobook at your favorite retailer.

# Also By The Author

## THE WITCH'S COVE SERIES, A PARANORMAL COZY MYSTERY SERIES

After weeks of dodging her grandmother's calls, Jo Maelstrom gets news that she died, and her cash-strapped supernatural dive bar and marina, Witch's Cove, is now hers. But when the leader of the local mermaid clan washes up dead on the shore, Jo finds herself embroiled in the question of who and why – and does it have anything to do with her own grandmother's mysterious death?

A Mer-Murder at the Cove is the first book in the Witch's Cove Paranormal Cozy Mystery series.

# About the Author

S. Usher Evans was born and raised in Pensacola, Florida. After a decade of fighting bureaucratic battles as an IT consultant in Washington, DC, she suffered a massive quarter-life-crisis. She found fighting dragons was more fun than writing policy, so she moved back to Pensacola to write books full-time. She currently resides there with her husband and kids, and frequently can be found plotting on the beach.

Visit S. Usher Evans online at:
http://www.susherevans.com/

www.ingramcontent.com/pod-product-compliance
Lightning Source LLC
Chambersburg PA
CBHW030538130726
48054CB00020B/90

* 9 7 8 1 9 6 5 7 6 7 3 7 5 *